"What happened out there, Summer?" Clay demanded.

He kept his gaze steady on her. "Can you go over it for me so you're ready with the details the police will need?"

"Who *are* you?"

"I told you. Clay Hitchcock, and I'm your brother's friend."

She shook her head. "I mean, who are you and why are you asking me questions like that?"

"I'm just someone who wants to help." That *was* the truth now. He may have the heart of a cop, the mind of a cop, but he was a civilian. His choice, yes, but it was still taking some getting used to.

Her eyes narrowed but she took his answer. Not, Clay noticed, because he had done anything to convince her that he was trustworthy. No, the only reason she was willing to entertain trusting him at all was the fact that her brother liked him.

He made a mental note about her character—family was important.

Not that he necessarily needed to make notes about Summer Dawson's charac

Still, his old habit of anal about them, died hard. H he was still a cop inside.

Sarah Varland lives near the mountains in Alaska, where she loves writing, hiking, kayaking and spending time with her family. She's happily married to her college sweetheart, John, and is the mom of two active and adorable boys, Joshua and Timothy, as well as another baby in heaven. Sarah has been writing almost since she could hold a pencil and especially loves writing romantic suspense, where she gets to combine her love for happily-ever-afters, inspired by her own, with her love for suspense, inspired by her dad, who has spent a career in law enforcement. You can find Sarah online through her blog, espressoinalatteworld.blogspot.com.

Books by Sarah Varland

Love Inspired Suspense

Treasure Point Secrets
Tundra Threat
Cold Case Witness
Silent Night Shadows
Perilous Homecoming
Mountain Refuge

Visit the Author Profile page at Harlequin.com.

MOUNTAIN REFUGE

SARAH VARLAND

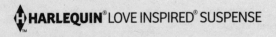

HARLEQUIN® LOVE INSPIRED® SUSPENSE

Recycling programs for this product may not exist in your area.

LOVE INSPIRED BOOKS

ISBN-13: 978-1-335-49020-9

Mountain Refuge

Which hope we have as an anchor of the soul, both sure and stedfast.
—*Hebrews* 6:19

To Elizabeth, my editor. I often think that the books should have both of our names on them for how much what you do impacts the story for the better. I love working with you, look forward to your comments and smile when I read an edited section we added to the book and can't remember if I wrote the addition or if you did. I had no idea when I started writing how much polish an amazing editor like you brings to a manuscript. Thank you for every single book.

ONE

Summer Dawson was alone on a mountain when she heard the first out-of-place sound, felt the first inklings that something might be wrong, that danger might be close.

She'd been running uphill, relishing the burning in her legs and lungs that reminded her that she was alive, when something rustling in the bushes made her pause and listen.

Summer had stilled immediately and stood now, listening to the sounds she'd grown up with. The Alaskan mountain was full of life, even at ten o'clock at night as daylight was starting to fade. She should have started this run hours earlier, and usually did. Her busy schedule working at the lodge didn't leave a lot of time for training, but mountain running was important to her, her outlet, her dream she didn't like to talk about.

A dream she'd mostly given up on.

But still, she ran the mountains because it was what she'd always done.

Today's run, like every Tuesday, was supposed to be up Hope Mountain, across Lupine Pass, then down Cook Mountain, where her sister, Kate, would be waiting for

her. From there, they'd drive back to Summer's car at
the Hope Mountain Trailhead. Neither would talk about
why Summer trained so hard when she didn't compete
anymore, not even at nearby Mount Marathon, but they
did the same routine every week. Like clockwork.

Until now. A shiver ran through her, followed by
goose bumps down her bare arms. She untied the jacket
she always wore around her waist, put it on and hoped it
was just the cold and the later-than-usual night that had
her spooked. Much as she tried though, Summer couldn't
deny that something about the rustle in the bushes had
her on edge. Her hand went to the bear spray attached
to the belt she always wore when she ran. The Kenai
Peninsula was known for its large brown bears. Summer had seen more than one in her time in the woods
but never too close. So far she'd escaped any encoun-
ters like that.

Hesitantly she moved forward again slowly, not wanting to run lest she awaken a bear's predatory instinct if
one did have her in its line of vision.

Then she heard nothing. Just the normal sounds. She
exhaled, picked up her pace slightly and removed her
hand from the bear spray.

And then something had her, from behind, hands on
her arms, rough, pulling, jerking her off the trail. She
heard a faint jingle, like car keys on a key chain maybe.
That was the sound she'd heard earlier—that's why she'd
been spooked. She opened her mouth and screamed, but
the deep humorless laughter behind her reminded her
how futile it was. This wasn't a well-used trail except
on weekends. No one would hear her screams.

"There's no use fighting. You're going to die today."

Summer tensed her arms, tried to wrestle out of his

grip, but he was too strong, even as he released her with one arm and then threw the other one all the way across her to pull her up against him, his hand heavy, her heart thudding in her chest.

Dying wasn't an option. Not for Summer. Not when for the last three years she felt like she'd barely lived. She'd gone through the motions, fulfilled obligations, even climbed mountains…

But she hadn't really lived. She wasn't ready yet, wasn't done.

No. Dying was *not* an option. She stilled slightly, hoping she could lull him into complacency, somehow trick him into loosening his grip so she could escape. Instead he held her against him even tighter, drew a knife with the other hand—he was left-handed, she should remember that—and ran it slowly up her arm. There was nothing remarkable about the knife except that it was large, four or five inches. Shiny. Sharp against her skin as he pressed just hard enough to leave the smallest of scratches.

"This is how it begins."

Something in the words sickened her, terrified her. *Please, God.* She didn't remember the last time she'd prayed. For now that was all she could muster.

Noise in the bushes startled them both. She felt her captor shift and assumed he was looking at the noise. She moved her head like she was too, but lowered her chin in the process. Took a breath and slammed her head back as hard as she could.

He yelled in pain, and when he loosened his grip slightly, she rammed an elbow into his ribs.

And then she was free.

Summer didn't stop to look back to see if he was pursuing—she just started running. She was free, she was alive and she had another chance to live like it.

She wasn't going to mess this up.

Clay Hitchcock pulled into the parking lot at the Moose Haven Lodge, hoping his fresh start wouldn't turn out to be a disaster. He was already later than he'd meant to be. A glance at the dash reminded him of that. It was 11:00 p.m. If Tyler hadn't assured him any time before midnight was fine he'd feel awful. As it was, Clay just felt tired. He jerked the key from the ignition, exhaled and got out.

Tyler Dawson, the friend who had gotten him this job, ran from the lodge. "I need your help."

"What's wrong?"

"My sister should have been back from a hike an hour ago."

"And she's not?" Cop senses died hard apparently, because Clay's instincts heightened, ready for action as if he was back in his old life.

"No. We're spreading out. If I give you directions, can you drive around a certain area?"

"Of course." Clay might be new here, but he did most of his growing up in the swamps and woods of coastal Georgia. Back roads were somewhere he felt comfortable.

"Here."

Tyler handed him a ripped strip of paper, like they'd written out a list of places to search and divided them up. Not bad for civilians running an informal search. Speaking of which… "You've called the police, right?"

"Yes. But we're a small town with a small department.

There are only three Moose Haven officers and one of them is out on maternity leave. So that leaves two."

Clay winced, knowing from his own police experience that the chances of both even being able to join the search were slim.

"They're both searching because one of them is my brother."

Clay whistled low. "Are you going out too?" He hadn't seen any other cars in the lot when he'd pulled up and had wondered if the lodge was empty this late at night.

"My truck's around back. Call me if you see anything and I'll let everyone else know."

Clay nodded, climbed back into his truck and drove away.

The woods alongside the roads he drove looked nothing like the tall Georgia pines he was used to investigating among, but the situation was familiar to him. He'd been involved in a search or two during his time at the Treasure Point Police Department, but even though he'd only been officially without a badge for two months now, it felt like a lifetime ago.

Unless Clay let himself actually remember it, hang on to that part of his life. And then it felt like yesterday. But he didn't want that. Couldn't take that.

He pulled out of the parking lot and looked at the note Tyler had given him. Howard's Landing Road was the first road, followed by a list of other locations and directions from place to place. He pulled the first road up on his phone's map setting and pressed the gas.

He realized as he drove that he hadn't asked which sister was missing. Tyler had two. Kate and Summer, if he remembered their names correctly from hearing

Tyler mention them in the past. Who was lost? What had happened?

God, we could use some help.

The words came easily. People had let him down in his lifetime, more in the last few months than usual, but God never had. More now than ever, Clay clung to that faith. Having walked away from everything else consistent in his life, God was all he had.

And this job, thanks to Tyler. Which wasn't off to the best start. What had happened to whichever Dawson sister was missing?

He continued praying silently as he drove, even as years of law enforcement thoughts crowded his mind, pushed out any hope of peace he had been clinging to. Odds weren't good that she was unharmed.

Clay hoped, whichever sister it was, she could take care of herself.

And hoped even more that God would take care of her.

Summer Dawson's feet pounded the dirt beneath them as she rounded another corner in the thick spruce forest, desperately struggling to stay ahead of whoever was behind her, whoever this man was who wanted her dead. She could still hear his footfalls, the rocks in the trail scattering behind her, and knew he wasn't far behind.

If only she knew how long she'd be running. She was in good shape, leading hikes at her family's lodge for so many years had seen to that, not to mention her training regimen—but she'd already been out for several hours. Fatigue wouldn't take long to set in, and Summer didn't know where she was—she'd had to divert from the path she knew after she'd rounded one of the corners and *he* had been there waiting.

Summer hadn't had time to react, hadn't had time to assess the situation or use any of the self-defense training or survival skills she possessed. In the moment when she'd needed all of that most, all she'd been able to do was scream. Finally she'd hit him hard enough to be able to run.

But first he'd been able to talk to her, say things she wouldn't soon forget. First, he'd been able to run a knife up her arm and promise her that death wouldn't come quickly.

Summer wondered if, when she stopped, when she'd gotten away and didn't have to run anymore, if she'd feel the cold blade against her skin like it was still there. Somehow she suspected she would.

Determination renewed, she pushed herself harder. She was less than ten miles from her family's lodge, she was fairly certain about that much. Summer didn't recognize the trail she was on right now, but it had to connect eventually to one she was familiar with, didn't it?

As she ran, Summer went over her would-be killer's description in her mind to make sure the details were cemented in her memory and to distract her from the burning in her lungs. He wore a mask. Black Carhartt stocking cap. She hadn't noticed much more than that, his features—the ones she'd been able to see—weren't etched into her mind the way the glimmering silver of the knife was.

Were it not for the noise in the bushes distracting him, Summer would probably be dead right now, bleeding out on the floor of the forest where she'd so often come to feel alive again. The irony wasn't lost on her. No, it cut deep inside, the pain so strong she almost couldn't bear it.

She'd felt safe here. And now that had been stolen from her.

Just like life had stolen so many things from her over the past three years.

She couldn't think about any of that right now, all she could afford to focus on was running, the fall of her feet, pushing harder, faster, as her lungs screamed for air. She silently chastised them. Better to be burning and in pain than dead.

Please, God… She'd prayed more tonight than she had since the night three years ago when everything had changed.

Summer didn't even know what she was praying for at this point. But she knew she needed all the help she could get.

She heard a twig snap behind her. Legs screaming, lungs burning, she sped up even more, one last sprint, that's all she had in her.

The woods grew lighter. Was that…?

There was a dirt road in front of her. A beautiful road that hopefully led to town. And people.

Still running, she whipped her phone out and used her voice-to-text feature to send a message to her siblings. Help. She wasn't willing to chance it by taking the time to say anything else, but she needed help. One of her brothers was a police officer in Moose Haven—she didn't know if they could GPS track her or anything, but it might be the only chance she had.

She emerged from the woods and ran into the road.

And almost ran straight into the path of a red pickup truck not fifty yards away, driving straight toward her.

Summer froze when she saw it, took only a second to make up her mind and then ran toward it, waving her arms. This couldn't be her attacker—he wouldn't have had time to get a truck to come after her, not when she'd heard his footsteps behind her only minutes before. It could be a getaway car, driven by another criminal, but it was a measured risk on Summer's part—it was more likely the driver was someone who could help her. Besides, she couldn't outrun a pickup, and if the driver of it wanted her dead, he'd just run her over while she sprinted down the road. Better to take a chance, maybe get out alive. Still, her heart pounded a crazy rhythm in her chest. How had her night gone from enjoying her usual route to this—running for her life? The driver stopped when she reached him, and she threw the door open.

"Drive."

Amazingly, he didn't ask questions. He just floored it down the road, eating up the gravel and throwing up dust.

TWO

Clay's world felt like it had gone from zero to sixty in less than ten seconds. He didn't know why he was so surprised he'd found Tyler's sister—at least he was pretty sure that was who he had found—because he'd prayed for that very thing. Still, seeing her dart into the road, clearly running from something, and jumping into his truck like she trusted him to protect her, it was overwhelming.

"Are you Summer Dawson?" he asked as he drove. He glanced down at his search directions and planned a quick route back to the lodge.

He caught her frown out of the corner of his eye. "Why?" she asked.

"Your brother has people out looking for you and I'm supposed to call if I find you."

"Which brother?"

"Tyler." Clearly he'd overestimated the amount of trust she'd have in a stranger. She needed to get out of her situation badly enough to jump in the truck, but now that she was momentarily safe, she was trying to keep herself that way by being guarded. Clay understood, but needed a way to convince her he wasn't a threat.

"My phone is on the dashboard. You can call Tyler from it if you want—you'll see that I have his number. He'll also confirm who I am if you ask him to. I'm Clay Hitchcock and I'm guiding at the lodge this summer."

She reached for the phone and pressed the screen a few times. Calling Tyler, he assumed.

"It's Summer. I'm safe and I'm with Clay, your friend?"

He didn't miss how that last part was a question. When he'd found out she was missing, he'd assumed that in this remote area of Alaska, she'd had a bad encounter with a wild animal or had issues with the terrain. The darker possibilities of meeting a human who wanted to cause her harm had crossed his mind, but he hadn't thought they deserved a great deal of consideration up here in this small, picturesque Alaska town and had written them off as paranoia. Now he wasn't sure. She was too upset, too skittish and hesitant to trust to have been running from an animal.

He stole a quick look at her and thought her frown had eased slightly. Good. With that tension on her side out of the way, he could focus on getting whatever information he could out of her about her encounter. He knew law enforcement would want to talk to her as soon as they got to the lodge, but it wasn't uncommon for the edge of a person's memory to fade the longer they were out of a traumatic situation. Maybe talking about it now would help cement some of the details in her memory.

"I'm okay for now, Tyler. I'll be okay, alright?"

Not a very convincing voice she was using, and Clay didn't blame her. Whatever happened had clearly been extremely traumatic for her to get in the car with a stranger when she was so shaken up.

"Alright, bye." She finished the conversation and set the phone down and looked back at him.

Clay kept his eyes on the road, though he could feel hers on him. After so many years in law enforcement, he was more used to being the one doing the assessing than the one being measured. Her stare disconcerted him.

"What happened out there, Summer? Can you go over it for me?"

"Who *are* you?"

"I told you, my name is Clay Hitchcock, and I'm your brother's friend."

"I mean, who are you and why are you asking me questions like that?"

"I'm just someone who wants to help." That *was* the truth now. He may have the heart of a cop, the mind of a cop, but he was a civilian now. His choice, yes, but it was still taking some getting used to.

Her eyes narrowed but she took his answer. Not, Clay noticed, because *he* had done anything to convince her that he was trustworthy. No, the only reason she was willing to entertain trusting him at all was the fact that her brother liked him.

He made a mental note about her character—family was important.

Not that he necessarily needed to make notes about Summer Dawson's character. After tonight they might only see each other in passing. Clay didn't remember what she did at the lodge, but with as many warnings as Tyler had given him not to think about dating one of his sisters, especially Summer, Clay felt it was safe to assume he wouldn't be assigned to any task that would lead them to cross paths often. But his old habit of analyzing people, observing things about them, died hard. He might not have a badge, but he was still a cop inside.

Maybe this was what the chief had tried to warn him about when he urged Clay to consider what he was doing by leaving the force in Treasure Point. But Clay hadn't listened, couldn't have. He'd needed to get out of there.

Out of that whole line of work.

He stole a glance at Summer. Much as he wanted to drive her back to the lodge and accept the no-trespassing sign she'd clearly placed in front of the details about whatever had just happened, he couldn't. Despite himself.

Clay let out a breath. "How do I get to the Moose Haven Police Department?"

"What?" The edges of her tone were sharp from fear or surprise, it was hard to say which—the two were often so intertwined.

"You're running from something," he explained, keeping his voice calm like he usually did when he was talking to a victim. "I'm assuming if it were an animal you wouldn't be so jumpy now that you're in a car and safe. I'd like to know what happened, but I don't need to. However, if I'm right about why you're running, the police do need to know."

Why hadn't Summer paid more attention when Tyler had talked about who he was hiring for work this season?

As this man, Clay, looked at her, she got the impression he knew her somehow better than he should. From Tyler? Or was he just that talented at reading people?

Summer didn't know, but she wasn't accustomed to such perceptive scrutiny, and didn't like it. She made herself not break his gaze though, saying without saying anything that she wasn't intimidated by him. Because she wasn't. He may be seeing her at her worst right now, but Clay needed to know she was no damsel in distress, no pushover.

Still, he had a point about going to the police. "Fine," she relented. "Turn left."

He did so. Then said "thank you" so quietly she thought maybe she'd imagined it. Now it was her turn to study him. Strong, solidly built, definitely attractive. And yet, he didn't seem pushy. Seemed steady, calm.

Actually he reminded her in some ways of her older brother Noah. He was the police chief of Moose Haven now, and at thirty was the youngest person to ever hold that role.

Clay had the same kind of bearing.

"You're a cop, aren't you?"

Clay glanced over, surprise on his face. She'd phrased it as a question but her tone had shown her certainty. He didn't confirm or deny her suspicions. Summer kept going.

"What are you doing in Moose Haven, really?" she asked without waiting for him to answer. His silence was confirmation enough. Summer shivered. Had he been fired from some police department, was that why he'd needed a new job? She'd heard stories about dirty cops, obviously, though she preferred to think they were the exception rather than the rule. Still, Clay's appearance right after she'd been attacked did feel a little co-incidental...

Her brothers would have confidently called it "God's provision." Such phrases hadn't slipped off Summer's own tongue comfortably for years.

"I'm working at the lodge, I told you."

"But you're not like the usual workers. You're different." The words slipped out before she could analyze them, decide if they could be read into at all. Summer left them hanging there, and didn't know what to make of it when Clay didn't comment.

They pulled into the parking lot of the small Moose Haven Police Department without any more conversation between them. Summer exited the car as fast as she could and headed toward the double doors at the front of the station.

Not until she heard a car door slam behind her and then footsteps catching up did it occur to her that Clay might be coming inside.

She mustered up the strongest, most take-charge voice she could find. "Listen, thanks for the ride, but I'm good. I can take it from here."

Was that a slight smile? "I'm sure you can," he agreed as he reached for one of the front doors and held it open for her. Summer frowned a bit before entering the building ahead of him. "But they're going to want to talk to me too."

"Why?"

"Because like I told you in the car, I suspect you're running from some*one*, not some*thing*. In that case, this is a crime or a potential crime and they're going to want to know where I was, how I found you, if I noticed anything. It's standard procedure."

It might have been, but Summer feeling like this certainly wasn't. She was already shaken up from the whole ordeal and now she just felt embarrassed by the way she'd treated Clay suspiciously, even after Tyler had managed to mostly convince her that he was one of the good guys.

"Fine." She didn't have anything else to say and ignored the tugs inside her heart urging her to apologize to Clay. She'd deal with those impulses later, but for now she wanted to stay focused on reporting what happened. It had been too long since she'd felt ready to move on with her life after what had happened in the past. Tonight she felt ready and she didn't want this to slow her down.

He followed her into the building.

"Summer."

Noah saw her before she saw him and swept her into a tight hug. Tyler was always the more demonstrative of her two brothers, so having Noah act this way surprised her. She hugged him back and tried not to shudder under the impact of realizing how deeply Noah had been worried. Her family had been her rock through all her troubles—she hated the thought of making them scared for her again.

"Come into my office." He looked in Clay's direction. "You too. Clay Hitchcock?"

Clay nodded and Noah gave him an approving smile. Any fears Summer had about him being on the wrong side of the law dissipated. To get past one of her brothers was difficult enough, but to get past both would be nearly impossible. Clay must be who he said he was.

Which left her really no reason to dislike him other than that she was still shaken up by him seeing her in such a vulnerable state—a state that had made her treat him rudely. It wasn't his fault she'd been attacked, wasn't his fault she'd learned several years ago that vulnerability with men was dangerous and to be avoided at all costs.

They went into Noah's office and sat down in the uncomfortable wooden framed chairs in front of Noah's desk. Noah went behind the desk, looking very officer-like and Summer felt a burst of pride in her brother. At least she knew he would do everything to find whomever had tried to attack her. The man who'd attacked her had really picked the wrong family to mess with.

"Why don't you tell me what happened?"

Summer did so, remembering all the details, which surprised her and the men also, judging by the looks on their faces. She even remembered to tell them that her attacker was left-handed.

"Not something that necessarily helps figure out who did it but it could help you narrow down a suspect list," Clay said so quietly Summer almost didn't hear. She was more convinced than ever that this was a job he was used to doing and surprised herself by hoping she'd get a chance to talk to him about it later. It didn't have anything to do with him, really, or how attractive he was in his quiet way. She was curious. That was all.

She swallowed hard.

"It'll be okay, Summer."

Noah thankfully mistook her expression for worry about the case, which it should have been, not angst over how tangled up her emotions felt from being rescued by this man, whether she wanted to be the type that needed rescuing or not.

"I hope so." She hoped *everything* would be okay.

"What did you notice?" Noah turned his attention to Clay, and Summer let herself relax a little. She hadn't meant to close her eyes, but when she heard the words *safe house* and her eyes popped open she realized she must have been nodding off. Her adrenaline was crashing, no doubt.

"What?"

"I think we need to take you to a safe house." Noah's words were firm and Summer widened her eyes even further, then started shaking her head.

"You can't be serious."

"Someone is after you."

"Someone *was* after me," she corrected. "I got away. That's the end of it…isn't it?"

"Why would she need a safe house?" Clay asked Noah. It didn't seem like he thought it was necessary, either. Good, maybe her brother was overreacting. Although, was it Summer's imagination or did she see something in Noah's expression? Something that implied a bigger issue he wasn't telling her?

"I have reason to believe it would be a good idea." Noah stood his ground.

Summer shivered. "Why don't you tell me what that reason is?"

Noah shook his head. "Summer, listen, you'd go away for just a few weeks, okay? We will do our best to get this solved…"

A few weeks of isolation during her favorite season, missing mountain running, her hikes with the tourists, time with her family… For what? Yeah, this man was dangerous—she definitely knew that. The police department would need to catch him before he harmed anyone else. But this had been a crime of opportunity. As long as she didn't make herself an easy target, there was no reason to believe this man would come after her again… Was there?

Not to mention, the thought of leaving town and going somewhere by herself made her seriously uneasy. She shivered at the memory of how alone and vulnerable she'd been when she'd run from her would-be killer. All she wanted right now was to go home and surround herself in comfort, familiarity and her siblings' love until she felt safe again. The idea of leaving her support network behind felt chilling and wrong.

"I'm not going to a safe house, Noah. You're going to have to figure something else out."

A few beats of silence passed.

"Let me see what else I can work out," Noah said slowly. "Summer, would you mind stepping outside with Officer Lee?"

She looked at her brother, looked at Clay and frowned a little, then looked back at Noah.

Then she nodded, stepped outside of the room with the other officer and shut the door. And hoped she might find an unlikely ally in Clay, that he'd be able to convince Noah to drop the safe house idea. Anything had to be better than that.

"You want me to do what?" Clay said on the off chance he might have heard wrong.

Noah repeated himself. "I'm going to have Tyler assign you to do everything Summer does at the lodge so you can follow her around, serve as a bodyguard and keep her safe."

Clay scrambled for words, managing to say, "You don't even know me." Had he really moved four thousand miles away from the only home he'd ever known for a fresh start only to be pulled back into the job he'd left behind?

"I know you're a good man. You come highly recommended by your friends in Georgia and by the police chief of the department where you used to work. We do a pretty extensive background check for people who work at the lodge. Alaska's a good place for people who are running from something, and summer employment especially can attract those types. I like to know who's working for my family. So I know a lot about you. And I know you're more than qualified for the job I want you to do."

Clay exhaled.

Noah kept his gaze on him steady. The man didn't seem easily phased, or easily dissuaded—a good quality in law enforcement. Something they had in common, at least according to people Clay had worked with before who had said the same thing about him.

"I want to shoot straight with you," Noah continued. "I'm not completely comfortable with turning this protection detail over to you. Nothing against you, but she's my sister and I don't want to trust anyone but myself to keep her safe. But I can't devote all my time to that and still do my job. And if I'm not doing my job, then the Moose Haven PD suffers and this guy might be able to keep operating longer with one less agency searching for him."

"But why me? Surely you've got other resources."

"Limited. You know how it goes in a small town. There's no proof that there's an ongoing threat against her and I only have a few officers. State troopers don't have a lot of manpower to spare down here, either—state cutbacks."

It had been months since anyone had counted on Clay for anything. Sixty days, almost exactly, since he'd officially worked his last shift in a police department. He met Noah's eyes, noting that the other man's look was serious, heavy with expectation. And Clay knew he was going to have to tell him no.

"Don't you think it's likely that this was a onetime thing—just Summer being in the wrong place at the wrong time? Our guy might have no idea who Summer is or where to find her even if he wanted to attack again. And protective details weren't what I signed up for. I came to help Tyler around the lodge." But the excuse sounded weak even to his ears. Clay winced at his own words.

Noah took them in stride. "Tyler won't mind. He wants Summer safe too. And…it may not be a onetime thing."

"What do you mean?" He heard something in the other man's tone. There was more to this story than overprotective brother syndrome.

"Anchorage Police Department has had a serial killer around the city for the last month and a half or so. Summer fits the age range, the general description—female, between ages twenty-five and early thirties, fit. I'm not entirely sure this isn't related to that."

"You think she was deliberately targeted by a serial killer—that he knew where to find her."

Noah grimaced. "It had barely crossed my mind as a possibility down here in Moose Haven until today. I knew about it, of course—it's been in the news and I try to keep track. But he hadn't left the Anchorage area, to our knowledge."

"What makes you think he has now?"

"Just the general similarities…gut instinct mostly, I guess."

"So are the troopers going to come investigate?" Clay had researched a bit about the local law enforcement agencies before he'd moved to Alaska, because even though he knew leaving the job behind with his old life was the best course of action, he couldn't quite give up the idea of returning to it one day.

"No. Not enough similarities for them."

"From what Summer told you, it sounds like a similar MO though?"

"Yes. I can show you the files for details, though it's not pretty."

"What's missing?"

"He usually kills in pairs. Not together necessarily, but two women in a short time span. Every time, it's been that way." Noah stood, paced toward the small window in his office, then returned to face Clay. "Listen, like I told the trooper I spoke to on the phone a few minutes ago, I just have a bad feeling about this."

"Better safe than sorry," Clay said without thinking, without realizing that he was essentially agreeing with Noah that Summer needed protection. Was all but offering to do it.

"How many women have been killed?"

"Six."

"Any survivors?"

"Not until Summer."

Six women dead. Clay would not let Summer be number seven. He exhaled. Nodded firmly.

"I'll do it."

THREE

The fire in the fireplace in the front room of the lodge danced and crackled, the only sound in the quiet. Summer walked toward it, enjoying the warmth. It might be summer, but nighttime in Alaska always carried a chill. It was past one in the morning now, and the sky was darkening into the twilight that would last for another two or three hours until the sun fully rose again. Summer shivered. From the darkness? From the cold? She didn't know, but she was more chilled than usual today, with the events of earlier on her mind.

She'd hoped telling the police about it would soften the details of the attack in her memory, but so far it hadn't worked. If anything, saying everything out loud had pushed the memories deeper into her psyche, on some track that repeated over and over, replaying like a bad movie.

She wasn't eager to go to sleep tonight. Summer felt the chances of reliving the attack in her dreams was too great a risk to take. She'd rather be tired.

She moved to the couch and picked up her sketchbook and a few pencils.

"You draw?"

She didn't turn as Clay's footsteps came closer. Emotions danced around inside her mind as she worked to settle on which one was strongest. Embarrassment, yes, that was it. Not only had she thrown herself into his path like some sort of damsel in distress, a role Summer wasn't used to playing and refused to play, but she'd been standoffish and prickly, something that also wasn't like her. Even Kate had said something to her about it earlier and Kate wasn't the warmest of people when you didn't know her.

She probably couldn't put off the necessary apology any longer, as it appeared Clay wasn't going away.

"I do." She set the pencils in her lap and shifted her weight a little so she'd be face-to-face with Clay, who stood near the couch, just on the edge of the room. "Are you going to sit?"

"Didn't know if you wanted company."

"Does what I want matter at this point?"

"You're still here at the lodge instead of in that safe house your brother picked out, aren't you?" His voice gave away what he thought about that.

Hadn't Clay backed her up earlier on the fact that a safe house wasn't necessary? His tone now seemed to indicate something had changed. What had that conversation between him and her brother been about?

"For now. And look, I'm sorry that messes up what you thought you'd be doing." Noah had informed her that Clay would basically be her bodyguard for the foreseeable future. She knew it wasn't Clay's fault, that he was just doing this because her brothers had asked him to, but the resentment was hard to repress. "It's not what I was expecting, either—I don't want my life arranged for me." She'd spent too much time and energy crafting five-year plans to have them yanked away because of an attack that could have just been random. So far there was no proof anyone would come after her a second time. Summer was hoping, even thinking of *praying*, that it was a onetime thing.

"I don't mind."

Such a quiet, calm answer. Summer didn't know what to do with that.

She exhaled. "Look, I'm sorry. About now and about earlier. You're not seeing my best side at the moment."

"Situations like this don't tend to bring those out in people."

"You've seen them before."

He didn't answer immediately. Just walked around the coffee table to the other end of the couch where she sat and took a seat. "I have."

"Tyler trusts you. That makes sense, you're his friend. But Noah trusts you too. You didn't answer me before, but I was right with my guess, wasn't I? You're law enforcement, aren't you?"

"No."

"But you were." His reaction to the question had made her even more sure, but it was more than that. It was the way he'd reacted when she'd first jumped in his truck—not overly riled but instantly understanding the seriousness of the situation. It was the way he'd listened as she told her story, the way he didn't seem overly excited by anything but at the same time seemed like he never fully relaxed, was always aware of their surroundings and ready to do his part to neutralize any threat.

"I was."

Summer liked that about him, the way he didn't give more answer than he had to at first but didn't attempt to dance around a direct question, either. A straight question deserved a straight answer. It seemed Clay agreed. A mark in his favor.

"I don't suppose you'd tell me…"

"Not at the moment."

The tone of his voice didn't change a bit, his expression didn't flinch. But the subject was clearly closed. Interesting. She was curious, not because she necessarily doubted his ability to protect her, although maybe there was a little of that. But she also just wanted to know.

"What do you think about the guy who's after me?" Somehow Summer felt that if she was quiet, he'd be the one asking the questions and she wanted to avoid that for now. As long as she was asking the questions, she was the one in control.

"We don't know enough yet to make any kind of guesses." He took a sip from the mug she hadn't noticed him carrying in with him. Coffee, she'd guess. Her siblings liked the stuff. Summer preferred tea—had gotten hooked on it one summer she'd spent in Europe mountain running and climbing.

"What do we know?"

"I'm not part of the investigation, Summer. I'm just looking out for you."

"Surely they've talked to you about why that's necessary."

"They have."

She let those words hang in the air for a minute while she considered them. "But you aren't telling me."

"Because right now, all we have are theories. They won't help you. They'll just drive you crazy thinking about the possibilities. I will tell you everything I know the second I think that's what is best for you."

Summer felt her shoulders tighten, the first hint of a frown on her face. He'd met her hours earlier. Who was he to decide what was best for her? She opened her mouth, ready to let him have it. Before she could say anything to him, she heard something. A doorknob being rattled? But everyone was inside already. They weren't waiting for anyone.

She stopped and sat up straight. "What was that?"

Clay was already on his feet, reaching out for her hand, and she took it, the fight she'd been meaning to pick just seconds before mostly forgotten. The doorknob wasn't making noise anymore, but in the seconds that had followed the initial rattling, there'd been a loud clatter, a small crash like one of the small tables on the porch had been knocked over.

Someone was outside.

"Go after him!" Summer urged.

"I can't. I have to stay with you." Clay had his phone out. "Noah, I think there's an intruder on the deck. Okay. Yes. That's what I thought."

He hung up. "This way." He pulled her toward the staircase that led to the upstairs guest rooms and some of the family's bedrooms. Two of those were upstairs—Summer's and Kate's—and Noah's and Tyler's were in another hallway off the main floor.

"You have to go after him," she protested even as she followed him. "He found me, he knows where I am. He's come after me twice now and it's just going to keep happening unless we face it and do something about it."

Clay whirled to face her. "This is what needs to be done right now, Summer. You need to be kept safe and you need to stop questioning the people trying to make that happen."

She didn't say anything else. Just continued up the stairs and entered her own room when he motioned her inside. It was more of a suite than a room, and the door opened into an area with a small couch, a coffee table and a drawing desk. Off that was the bedroom and bathroom.

She stopped just inside the door. "What now?"

"Sit down and wait."

Summer did it, fighting frustration. And maybe…

Was that fear?

Out of all her siblings, Summer considered herself one of the most fearless. Noah and Tyler weren't overly afraid by any means, but they didn't seek out danger the way she and Kate always had. Noah becoming the police chief had actually surprised the rest of them, but he'd explained that he'd rather face danger every day if it meant he was doing something to protect the rest of the town from it. Kate was an adventurer like Summer, but she acknowledged danger, didn't mind staring it in the face. Summer? Summer didn't usually notice danger. Her favorite place in the world was up on top of a ridgeline, running on it as her heart pounded, adrenaline rushing through her body, and dancing over rocks at what always felt like the tippy-top of the world.

There was no room for fear.

So this wasn't a feeling she was used to. Then again, she also wasn't used to losing her sense of control. Sure, there was a point in the run downhill when you had to lose a bit of your control and hope you didn't end up hitting the small, loose rocks of the scree too many times and getting too scraped up. But even then, it was a voluntary surrender of control, for the sake of the race, the run, the exhilaration.

This was control that someone was trying to take from her. Summer balked at that.

"I'm not going to keep running. I hope he knows that. I hope he knows—"

"Shh." Clay had moved to the window and was looking out, watching what was going on outside.

"What's going on?"

"Noah and Tyler are both out there. A trooper car just pulled up and a woman got out."

"Erynn. She works with Noah sometimes." Her brother's opposite in so many ways. Watching the two of them interact was a favorite amusement for most of the people who knew them. "No sign of anyone…who shouldn't be here?" It was two in the morning but even as far south as Moose Haven, there would still be workable daylight—sort of a dark twilight—at this time of night in early summer.

"Not that I can see. They're coming inside now. We'll wait here. Noah knows where to find us."

"He sent you up here?" In the moment she hadn't even thought to wonder how he knew exactly where her room was.

Clay nodded. "He thought it was the most secure place for us to get to. And he's right. It'd be almost impossible for someone to get in here undetected."

"Almost?"

"Can't promise anything with 100 percent certainty," he said with a shrug, like he was used to people taking his control away. But then again, Summer guessed he was. She doubted there was ever a "normal" day for someone in law enforcement. Noah hadn't had to deal with as much since Moose Haven was usually a relatively quiet town—hunting violations and speeding tick-

ets were usually the craziest things her brother dealt
with, as far as Summer knew. Until this. Until today.

Someone knocked on the door. "It's me." Noah's voice.

Clay unlocked it and Noah came in, followed by Tyler
and Kate.

"He was here."

Summer had never heard Noah's voice like this. Hard.
Angry.

"How do you know?" Clay asked.

Noah glanced at Summer. Shook his head slightly,
like doing so would make her not aware of the fact that
he was trying to communicate without her noticing.

"I can handle it, Noah."

"You don't need to know," Noah insisted, Tyler and
even Kate nodding. She'd have to give her sister a hard
time later. The two of them had always stuck together
as kids whenever their brothers turned bossy or overprotective. Boys against girls and all that.

"I think she does," Clay said.

Summer swung her gaze to her unlikely ally, eyebrows raised, sure her surprise must be showing on her
face.

"You've read the reports," Noah said to Clay as if
she wasn't even there. She decided to let it go for now
and just listen.

"I have. And I think it's unfair to keep so much from
her when it's her life that's in danger. We're asking a
lot of her to do what people say without understanding
the situation, especially people like me who she doesn't
know or have any reason to trust."

More than the usual amount of pause dragged out.
Clay stood firm, Summer noticed, his posture giving
no indication that he was backing down. She'd never

thought she'd see someone willing to stand up to both her brothers, but here Clay was taking them on, plus Kate.

It was…nice.

"Alright." Noah looked to Summer. "You want to know?"

She wanted to go to sleep, wake up and realize it had all been a dream. With that not being an option… "Yes, I want to know."

"He was here."

"Who is *he*? You keep talking about him like he's someone else. Someone…specific. Do you have a suspect?"

"Not a name."

"But…?"

"I have reason to believe it may be the serial killer who's been killing women in Anchorage."

Summer's mind couldn't process, wouldn't wrap around what her brother had just said. "You think…?"

"The MO is incredibly similar."

"Surely if that were true I'd need more security than just Clay, right? No offense, Clay, it's just that I've seen the news articles about that killer. People haven't stood a chance against him." She waited for their answers.

No one said anything.

Until Clay finally spoke. "The problem is," he began, and for the first time Summer admitted to herself that the slow Southern accent calmed her, maybe just a little bit. It was easy to listen to him talk when she wasn't feeling her independence threatened with everything he said. "The MO doesn't fit perfectly. So we're waiting to see if this is just our suspicion or if it's founded."

"*Our* suspicion?" Noah asked Clay. Summer wasn't sure what to make of that. Had Clay disagreed at first?

Clay nodded. "I don't feel good about this."

Noah's face seemed to indicate that he agreed. "We'll investigate more outside tomorrow. For tonight I'll stay up and keep watch."

"I don't think I can sleep," Summer said.

"You can and you need to." Tyler pulled her into a hug. "Take care of yourself."

Summer hugged him back. It was possible she had the best brothers in the world. "I'll try." She offered a small smile.

"Good night." Kate smiled at her, but didn't offer a hug. She wasn't the huggiest of people, even with those she loved, so Summer didn't mind.

She smiled back. "Good night."

And then her siblings dispersed, leaving only her and Clay.

She turned to face him, not sure what to say. At first, she'd disliked him because she'd been embarrassed. Then it had been convenient to ignore him because she hadn't wanted his presence infringing on her independence, one of the things Summer held the most dear these days.

Now...

Summer wasn't sure. But she owed him a thank-you for convincing her siblings to see reason and to keep her in the loop.

"Thanks for getting him to talk to me," she offered softly, sighing after she did so. "I'm not the youngest, Kate is. But for whatever reason if someone needs extra care, they always assume it's me."

"Siblings are well-meaning but I hear they can be smothering."

"You have siblings?"

Clay shook his head. "I've got a friend who's about

as close as you can get, but no, not really. Must have been nice growing up with friends around all the time."

Summer couldn't argue with that.

"Listen, they are right though—you need to sleep."

"I can't sleep up here." So far from everyone else, with no easy escape route. At least downstairs had multiple routes to the outside. Here in her room it was the door or the window. She felt trapped and exposed at the same time.

"It's the safest place for you, Summer. Like I said earlier, it's all tucked back here so that you're almost impossible to get to."

She wouldn't sleep a wink. But if he was going to push the issue, she'd sit up and read all night.

"Alright," Summer said without further fight.

Clay moved toward the door. "I'll be right outside in the hall." Then he turned toward her, his eyes focused and thoughtful. "You aren't planning to even try to sleep, are you?"

"Not even a little."

He laughed. A real, actual laugh. "May as well head downstairs, then. Maybe you'll nod off on the couch."

Summer followed him down the stairs, his laughter echoing in her mind, almost pushing away the niggling fears that reminded her that someone wanted her dead.

Almost.

But not quite.

Clay didn't know what had gotten into him earlier, snapping at Summer when she'd tried to tell him to go after the guy. He could count on one hand the number of times in his adult life he'd lost his temper. He had his own struggles, wouldn't say he was 100 percent the man he wanted to be, but temper wasn't usually one of his issues. It disconcerted him that fear for Summer's safety, combined with him being upset over her persistent stubbornness, had made him lose it like that.

He looked over at her stretched out across the couch, eyes closed. Clay had tried to convince her that her room was actually safer, tucked away and on the second floor, but she hadn't listened, just like she hadn't listened to her brother when he'd brought up the idea of the safe house earlier.

She was stubborn. On one hand, the stubborn ones usually survived when they were attacked, something Summer had already proved true in her first and hopefully only encounter with the attacker. On the other, the stubborn ones were bad about taking precautions and following advice—something Summer had also proven. She clearly wasn't going to listen to anyone, even when it would be wise, if it went against what she thought.

Clay exhaled.

This wasn't what he'd wanted from his fresh start in Alaska. He'd known Tyler's brother was in law enforcement, but he hadn't expected to have any part in it himself. Not that he blamed them for asking for his help. It was the logical choice, Clay just wasn't sure he was ready for it, wasn't sure he trusted himself to have the instincts he used to have, before he'd started to doubt himself.

But he owed it to his friend to try to keep his sister safe.

And doing that, he was seeing now, also probably meant he couldn't keep his distance, not even emotionally. The Dawson family needed as many people as they could get on their side convincing Summer to listen to whatever recommendations law enforcement made—and he wouldn't be able to do that unless they were something resembling friends.

He glanced at her again while she slept.

It wasn't that being Summer's friend would be unpleasant. He admired her strength, her spunk, was intrigued by her and thought she was beautiful. Maybe those things were the problem. He had to think of her as a *friend* only, nothing more, because it was all she could possibly be. He wasn't staying in Alaska long. He was friends with her brother. Reasons to keep his caring on a friend level and not allow it to go any further ran through his mind like facts on a ticker board.

The biggest one was that he wasn't an emotional kind of guy. He kept emotions out of his work life and he'd been a good cop, the possible exception being that last case that even his chief insisted he couldn't have seen coming. Besides that, he'd always done a good job keeping a cool head, staying logical and by the book. Letting himself get any closer to Summer might not allow him to detach the way he needed to in order to keep his focus sharp, keep his senses on alert.

Something he desperately needed to do. Because tonight he felt in his own gut the sinking feeling Noah had seemed to feel in his. Something about this ongoing menace toward Summer felt weightier, more heavy with evil than a random attack. Clay was almost sure Summer *was* the target of a serial killer. One who had been successful six times so far. Who would feel he'd been robbed of his seventh victim and would likely keep coming back until he could kill her too.

And it would be up to Clay to stop him.

FOUR

"Clay, you need to see this."

Tyler's voice.

Clay blinked his eyes open, exhaustion impossible to deny after the small amount of sleep he'd managed the night before. At least it had been more than anticipated— he'd planned to stay awake all night, but Tyler had come in around three thirty in the morning and told him he'd be awake doing lodge business and promised to wake him if anything happened. Clay had argued at first, but when Tyler insisted that Clay wouldn't do them any good exhausted, he finally gave in.

He sat up and glanced at his watch. It was 6:03 a.m. He slid his feet back into his boots, which sat beside the couch he'd slept on. Easy access. He wanted to know he could be ready at a moment's notice. He glanced at the other couch in the room, where Summer had fallen asleep last night, though he'd known she wouldn't be there. Kate had come down and finally convinced her to go up to her room somewhere around 3:00.

"What is it?" Clay was up and following Tyler in seconds, as Tyler walked toward the front door. Clay's eyes went to the stairs. "Is Summer okay?" He needed to know.

"She's fine. Sleeping, thankfully. She doesn't know about this yet and I'm not sure she needs to."

Clay understood Summer's siblings were only trying to protect her, but he disagreed with their methods. He didn't plan to keep anything from her permanently, at least not as it related to the investigation, though he supposed he could see some value in carefully choosing the timing for revealing information to her. There were things about himself he might keep from her, but only because that *was* truly for her own good. It was in both of their interests that he keep his distance from her, be her friend on only the most basic level. Acquaintance, really. An acquaintance tasked with keeping her safe. And nothing more.

"Did we miss something last night?"

"I'm not sure. But look."

Tyler pointed up at the front of the lodge. At first, Clay didn't see anything, just the wide log beams and siding that made up the lodge. He looked toward Summer's window.

There.

The window itself was outlined in red. Spray paint, Clay assumed, from the tint and the lack of drip pattern on the logs. Underneath the window, above the slant of the house's roof, were the words, YOU'LL BE EVEN MORE BEAUTIFUL WHEN YOU SLEEP IN DEATH.

"What...?" Clay clenched his fists and fought the childish desire to kick at the gravel rocks at his feet.

"I know." The anger in Tyler's voice reminded Clay he wasn't alone in his feelings, and that of the group of people worried for Summer's safety, he'd known Summer for the shortest amount of time. If he cared this much about keeping her alive, her family must be stressed beyond all reason.

"And you checked on her this morning?"

"Before and after I saw this, just to be sure. Yes, she's fine."

Clay exhaled. That reassurance did a little to calm him, at least. He pictured Summer as she'd been last night on the couch, eyes closed. Her face had stayed tense though, as if she wasn't able to relax, not even in sleep. Was that only because of the threat against her? he wondered. Or did it have to do with something else?

He didn't know her well enough to ask. Never would, he reminded himself.

"This isn't right." Clay walked down the parking lot a little, parallel to the lodge, looking at the painted words. "He was just trying to kill her and now he's leaving notes?" He shook his head, pulled his phone out of his pocket and called Noah. He didn't see the man's squad car in the parking lot so he assumed he'd already gone to work, probably hoping there'd been a break in the case or that looking at the notes with fresh eyes would help him *make* a break.

"Noah, someone was at the lodge last night after we were outside investigating, sometime after 2:30. Did you see his handiwork painted on the wall?"

"No. It was light when I got up but I was focused on making sure the perimeter was secure before I left, not looking at the whole place. What happened?"

Clay read the message to him.

Noah seemed to consider it. "As far as we know the serial killer in Anchorage hasn't left notes, either before *or* after the victims' deaths, so at least that's good news."

"You don't think it's him anymore?"

Noah let out a breath. "I may have been hasty to assume it was. I don't know yet. I want security around her just as tight as though he is the threat though. I'll be back to process the scene. Give me about thirty minutes. We'll talk more then. There are things I'd rather not say over the phone."

"Alright, see you then." Clay hung up the phone, turned his attention back to the message, looked over at Tyler who was still staring at the wall too, then focused back up at the chilling words.

"We figure out why he did this, we might figure out more about him," Clay thought aloud, considering the message, the placement of it, the logistics of leaving it. "He had to climb up there," he observed. "You keep a ladder near here?"

Tyler nodded. "Around the side of the lodge."

Clay headed in the direction the other man had indicated. Tyler started to follow but Clay stopped him. "You stay there. Don't let your sister's window out of your sight."

"Why shouldn't he let my window out of his sight?"

Clay jumped at Summer's voice in front of him. She'd come from around the side of the lodge, down a stone path that Clay guessed led to the back door.

"How much did you hear?"

Summer raised her eyebrows. "So I was right. You wouldn't have let me out here for some reason."

Tyler had mentioned checking on her. At that time, had he told her to stay in her room? It seemed likely. But even Clay knew that telling this woman to stay put would just make her curious about what she wasn't supposed to see. Tyler should have known it would make her come right outside.

"I didn't say that. But you're supposed to stay where you're put so we can try to keep you safe."

"Stay where I'm put?" Clay wouldn't have said her eyebrows could get any higher, but apparently that would have been wrong. Her shoulders squared, her chin lifted.

Frustration at the morning built inside Clay, but he took a breath to keep his temper in check. Most of the frustration he was feeling was aimed at Summer's attacker and Summer didn't deserve the brunt of that, even if she did seem determined to make his life harder by making her life more dangerous. Somehow though, he was beginning to understand her family's tendency toward being overprotective. Summer was so strong, brave. So independent. And maybe…maybe Clay just didn't want her to have to be all those things all the time if she didn't want to be. Because while it was clear she didn't want to be coddled, somewhere in her blue eyes he'd caught the smallest hint of vulnerability that made him think part of her *did* want protection, wanted to lean on someone, but didn't feel she should. It made him curious about her, made him want to know her more.

Something he needed to ignore, *would* ignore if he had any sense. For both of their sakes.

Her eyes went to the window and grew wide. "Why? Why would anyone do that?"

Clay admired how quickly she'd asked the question that had come to his mind. Motive was one of the key elements in solving any crime, and in a crime that could be related to a serial killer—he wasn't ruling that out yet, even if Noah sounded uncertain—it would be one of the hardest things to figure out. But once they had, understanding motive could be key to unmasking who was behind all of this.

"I don't know. It's something we're going to try to figure out today."

Was it his imagination, or did she edge closer to him? Not that he blamed her. She'd withstood more than the average person could take, pressure-wise, in the last several hours. Everybody had a breaking point. While it didn't look like they'd found Summer's yet, Clay knew they had to be careful.

She leaned closer to him and he searched for words to reassure her. "Stop looking at me like that," she whispered, her eyes meeting his. She held his gaze for a long span of seconds, then backed away.

And he'd thought she needed encouragement.

This woman wasn't going to stop surprising him with her strength, was she?

"Here's what we're going to do," Clay stated. "I'm going to sit here until Noah comes. It's unlikely he'll return to the scene, at least right now, but I'm not going to risk the evidence being compromised."

"You think the guy who did this could have left something behind that could help us ID him?"

Clay didn't want to give her too much hope, but then again, wasn't hope one of the things that made Christians different from people who didn't believe? He had to remember that. "It's possible. I can't promise anything."

Summer looked at him...funny. "No one can, Clay. No guarantees in life, I get that."

Once again, she'd surprised him.

"Anyone hungry?"

Tyler's abrupt question was out of place, but Clay recognized it as an attempt to break up the private conversation between himself and Summer. He stepped back, almost without realizing what he was doing.

"I'll go get some breakfast," Summer volunteered. Did she understand what Tyler was doing too and was going along with it, or was she just eager to eat? "I'll bring it out and we can picnic outside. Make the best of things, right?" She gave a small smile that seemed like a peace offering. She was still feisty this morning, stronger than almost any woman Clay had ever met, but she seemed softer around the edges somehow, at least with him. Like she'd determined maybe they should tolerate each other as long as they were going to be in such close proximity for the time being.

Toleration was fine, as long as it stayed professional. The more he learned about her, the more he needed reminders not to get too close.

He was leaving Alaska at the end of the summer. Tyler knew that, had been fine with it. Whether that had factored into his warnings to leave his sisters alone, Clay wasn't sure. But he'd made no secret of the fact that this wasn't a permanent trip. Of course, he had no idea where he was headed from there. Georgia still didn't seem right. It had changed in too many ways and he...hadn't.

Maybe Arizona. He'd never seen the Southwest and had always wanted to see the Grand Canyon.

But staying in Alaska wasn't likely. There was nothing for him here, except for a job that would only last over the course of the season. And anyway, Clay probably wasn't the settling-down type. It would be better to stay on his toes, keep moving, than have life come crashing down again in any way similar to what it was like when his parents died.

"You'd better not," he finally answered Summer. "I need you to stick close to me."

"I'm starving," she stated flatly.

"I'll bring breakfast out," Tyler offered, having walked back close enough to hear them. He looked at Clay. "Since you have to keep an eye on the scene."

He saw the warning in his friend's eyes. Message received. Clay nodded.

Tyler studied him for another second, then glanced at Summer. He shook his head slightly and walked away.

Great. Now Tyler was seeing things that weren't there.

Clay looked back at the writing on the house, thought about the case and tried to puzzle out why someone was after Summer in the first place. He knew there was no guarantee it was the Anchorage serial killer. In fact, he hoped for the sake of Summer's safety that it wasn't, because the guy was creepy good at what he did. Clay had spent some time searching online last night while he watched Summer sleep and kept an ear open for any suspicious activity.

He'd killed six women in the span of two months. Always two at a time, not necessarily together although once he'd done that, but within about four hours of each other. There was nothing too obvious that tied the pairs of victims together besides their basic demographic. They were women, all in their twenties and early thirties. Slim, athletic. All blonde.

Summer fit the profile. But Clay understood Noah's hope that she hadn't caught the serial killer's eye.

Besides, Summer was the only victim, or attempted victim that they knew of this time. While it was possible the killer would have moved locations and started targeting women on the Kenai after largely sticking with women in the Anchorage area, it wasn't likely he'd also change his MO enough to stop killing them two at a time.

So if they weren't dealing with a serial killer, then the attack against her must have had some other motive. Come to think of it, even if they *were* dealing with the serial killer, there were still questions about motive that needed to be answered. Why here? Why Summer? What about her had caught this killer's eye? To figure that out, he needed to know more about Summer.

"So tell me about yourself."

Summer's eyebrows raised. She laughed a little. "What?"

Clay realized he'd said nothing aloud for the past few minutes. No wonder Summer was confused. But the more he thought about the situation, the more he realized the opportunity they had. There were few leads on the killer because none of his targets had survived… until now. While the files for the other victims had been examined carefully for connections, the authorities were still at a loss to explain how the killer found his victims, and why he chose to attack.

Maybe having a survivor could help uncover answers.

"Say the guy after you is the serial killer."

"Um, I'd rather not."

"I mean, if he is. Assume for now that he is until we get another lead. It's all we have to work with and we should be as careful as if it were for sure true."

"Okay, I'm following."

"If it is the serial killer, then finding links between you and the other women…the ones he did, uh…"

"You don't have to sugarcoat it for me, Clay."

Hearing her say his name did weird things to his insides. He wanted to roll his eyes at himself. Please. Was he a fifth-grade boy with a crush or an adult man who knew when things were and were not a good idea?

"The women he killed have things in common. That's how serial killers work—they have a pattern, a type if you will, and they're after them for a certain reason. Sometimes it's because they remind the killer of someone in their past they were obsessed with for one reason or another. Sometimes the victims have something else in common the killer wants to make a statement against. Sometimes it's just people who the killer happened to have access to, because of where he lived, or what he or they did professionally. There are all kinds of options. I think because of the physical similarities in the women who have been killed—and you also—there's a good chance that's the link between the women. But in case there's more to it than that, I think finding out more about you and more about them might be a good way to figure out who's behind this."

"In that case…" Summer began.

"What?" he asked.

She hesitated. Studying him, weighing him, like she was trying to decide to what degree he was on her side.

"If that's the case, then maybe I could talk to some of the victims' families? See if there's anything else I have in common with the other women who were attacked?"

Clay's heart fell to his stomach. She was asking to get involved in the case in a more proactive way. The urge to take charge and actively fight against this guy was something he understood, but had hoped wouldn't happen for her. For one thing, if Summer insisted on being more involved, Clay would have to be too, something he would rather avoid. He'd made the choice to leave that life behind.

Besides that, he did want Summer safe and he knew that the chances of being able to keep her safe diminished if she insisted on taking an active role.

It was with that in mind that he said his next words. "I'm not so sure that's a good idea."

"You're not going to start sounding like my siblings are you?"

Maybe he was.

"Explain why you don't think it's a good idea." She said the words like she meant them, like she really cared about his thoughts.

Summer was trying to see Clay's point of view just like she was trying to see her siblings'. Really, she was. And it wasn't that she was brave or ignorant of the danger she was currently facing, but she'd never been one to sit still and wait for life to happen. She was the one who ran up mountains, across ridgelines.

She'd been accused more than once of looking for trouble, and while she disagreed with that assessment, she didn't go out of her way to avoid risk. It wasn't her style.

Life was too short to be lived half-heartedly. Summer had always believed that and still did now, despite the fact that she'd shifted her priorities in the last couple of years, more toward family and away from some of the selfish dreams she'd had when she was younger.

"Summer, the safest thing for you is to lay low while we figure out who attacked you. Proactively going and talking to other victims' families isn't that."

"Right, I can see that, but if I'm helping solve the case faster, isn't it for the best?"

Tires crunched the gravel in the driveway. Noah

parked and walked over to them. Summer's stomach growled. Tyler sure was taking his time with breakfast.

"Glad you're here." Clay stuck out his hand and Noah shook it. Something about the scene made Summer smile. Her brother liked Clay, something that couldn't be said for most men.

Not that it mattered to Summer. She'd tried romance before, and it had cost far too much. She'd almost lost her family, and she wasn't going to risk that again. No matter how great a man seemed at the beginning, there was no telling with her judgment.

"I'm going to go see what's taking Tyler so long with breakfast."

"You shouldn't be alone," Clay insisted. Summer looked to Noah.

Noah shrugged. "We'll both be right out here so it's probably alright. Don't be long, okay?"

Summer jogged easily to the stairs of the deck and ran up and inside. She found Tyler in the kitchen, icing some cinnamon rolls.

"Oh yum, where did those come from?"

"They were in the freezer. I warmed up a couple. Sorry it took so long."

He set down the icing bag and looked at her a little funny.

"What is it?"

"You seem to mind Clay a lot less today."

Was it her imagination or was Tyler not as thrilled by that as Summer would have guessed?

"I guess I felt like I was kind of a jerk to him yesterday. I'm trying to make up for it."

"Just don't try too hard."

"Why?"

"Because you two wouldn't be good for each other."

The absurdity was so great Summer just laughed. "Tyler, someone is trying to kill me. The last, and I do mean the very, very last thing I am thinking about is getting into a relationship with someone."

"Clay's not the kind of guy to do anything half-heartedly." There he went, the caution in his voice still strong. "If he falls for you, he'll fall all the way, Summer. I don't want you to hurt him and I don't want him to hurt you."

This conversation was giving her a headache. "I thought I should be nicer today. That's all."

"I just wanted to make sure—"

"Listen, message received, Tyler. I don't flirt with every male I come into contact with, okay? I was just trying to be friendly."

She took the plate of cinnamon rolls he handed her, though she doubted she'd eat more than a bite or two—her appetite was suddenly not as large as it had been a few minutes ago.

"Summer, I didn't mean—"

But she'd already left the house, wishing she could step away from the thoughts he'd put in her head just as easily. The truth was that Clay Hitchcock was attractive, sure. She'd noticed yesterday in the truck when he'd rescued her. She wasn't blind. But today she'd truly only been trying to make peace for the sake of making the next few weeks more tolerable. She knew better than her brother did how much she needed to avoid a relationship for now. Or the next few years. Or forever.

Still, it hurt to know that no matter how much she'd changed, how much she'd said she was sorry for hurting them, for not considering the reach of her choices, her family didn't truly believe she'd changed.

Her mistakes might not require her to wear a literal scarlet letter like Hester Prynne had in the book she'd been forced to read in high school, but in this small town and this family, they may as well. There was no escaping what had happened. She'd forever be the sister who had pushed her family away and run off with a man who didn't deserve her love, trust or innocence.

Years later and she'd asked forgiveness from everyone she'd hurt. God included, most of all. In return, she'd gotten an outpouring of love and acceptance. But that couldn't actually erase what had happened, or the damage it left behind.

No one seemed to be able to let it go and really put it in the past.

If she were honest…?

Herself included.

Holding the plate of cinnamon rolls, she hurried down the stairs from the front deck. "Breakfast."

Clay frowned. Summer knew he was too perceptive to have missed the shift in her attitude in the last ten minutes. Whatever, it wasn't something she could deal with discussing right now. He'd have to stay curious about what had come over her.

Noah and Clay each took a cinnamon roll. Summer took the one that was left over and nibbled at the edges of it. Moose Haven Lodge's cinnamon rolls were practically famous, so she couldn't resist them, no matter what kind of mood she was in.

"Did you find anything?" she asked her brother.

Noah shook his head. "Nothing Clay hadn't already thought of or found just by looking at it."

"Because there wasn't anything to find?"

"Because Clay's that good at this job." Noah eyed him. "After the summer, if you stay in Moose Haven I'd like to talk to you about a job. The city is increasing our budget for next year and adding you to the force would be money well spent."

"I appreciate you saying so."

He didn't respond any further to the suggestion. Interesting, at least to Summer. Was he not planning to stay in town? It wasn't uncommon for people to come up to Alaska to work only during the summers, but it still surprised her a bit anyway. Or maybe it had more to do with the offer of the job in particular?

"What we did learn is that both of us agree on the 'why' you were asking about earlier," Clay offered.

"And what did you decide?"

Noah spoke up. "It's odd for someone to try to kill you and then de-escalate, essentially, to trying to scare you. With that in mind, the only logical motive is that he wanted to unnerve you, keep you off balance, basically scare you as a tactic to feel like he still has you under control."

"Why would he do that? Just because he's mentally unstable?"

"It's not that simple," Clay replied. "We can't guess anything about his mental state besides the fact that he has a disregard for human life. Some serial killers are mentally unstable for sure. And some are people who seem to have all their faculties and then just…snap."

"Did you get a lot of serial killers where you're from?" Summer couldn't help the snarky comment as she hadn't really wanted to hear any of Clay's opinions. She trusted her brother.

"We got more crime than you might expect." Something in his face had changed, hardened, and Summer knew she'd crossed some kind of line—she hadn't expected her words to affect him to the degree they had.

"Besides," Clay continued, "the FBI-led academies I've been to, the conferences I've learned at, all of which have taught me plenty, thanks."

It appeared two of them could play the "let's be short with each other now" game.

Summer exhaled. Why was she doing this? Just because of a little goading by her brother? She should know better.

"I'm sorry."

Noah looked at her oddly and she shook her head slightly. Better to drop it and try to be normal around Clay, at least to the best of her ability.

"So that's why you think he's doing this?" Summer tried to redirect the conversation.

Clay looked to Noah to answer, apparently sensing that Summer was taking him more seriously. She felt bad about that. The truth was that she trusted Clay's opinion a great deal and didn't want to.

"That's the working theory."

"And do you think it's the serial killer or not?"

"No."

"Yes."

The two men answered at the same time. Noah's answer was more reassuring…

But Summer felt somewhere inside that Clay's was probably right.

"What do *you* think?" The question came from Clay.

Summer had to take a minute to compose herself before she reacted to his question. Had her expression given away that she agreed with him or had he just really wondered what she thought?

"I think it's him." She exhaled as she voiced the words she'd hoped to keep inside. Something about saying them out loud made the threat seem more real.

"Why?"

Now she knew he was interested in what she thought. With that in mind, Summer considered her answer carefully.

"Just the way it felt when he had me, with the knife…" she began. Images flashed in her mind and she squeezed her eyes shut tight for a second. Gut instinct said to push the images away, to try to forget about them, but Summer made herself focus on them instead, hopeful that some detail would stand out that she hadn't noticed before. Anything that would help them make progress in this case. Because if someone was after her, she wasn't going to sit around and hide. She was going to do something about it.

"I've got my team working on it and I've also alerted the troopers." Noah's words were meant for reassurance, but they could only do so much. Nothing changed the fact that someone was after her.

"Thanks."

"I'll keep you posted on what I learn today, alright? Thanks for telling me as much as you did yesterday. I've got some calls in, and a forensic artist in Anchorage is doing a full body sketch today based on the description you gave me."

"I didn't notice much." At least, Summer wouldn't have expected it would be enough to help.

"You'd be surprised what those guys can do with just a little bit of information," Noah said. "It doesn't always give an exact picture, but often it's close enough that someone recognizes them."

"Let us know," Clay said.

Noah nodded. "I'm going to climb up there, process the message for evidence and then head back to work. What are your plans?"

"I'd hoped to take the tourists who arrived last night on a hike," Summer said.

"No."

"Noah, this is my job."

"And no job is worth your life."

Summer knew that but also didn't think Noah understood how important her job at the family's lodge was to her.

Or why. But that was understandable. She tried not to talk about the *why*, tried not to think about it.

"I understand you want to keep me safe. Believe me, I want that too, but I can't stop everything because of some what-ifs."

"Someone has already grabbed you and then tracked you down to threaten you. I hardly think anything we are considering in any arena is as far-fetched as a what-if at this point. It's just what is, Summer. Someone wants you dead."

"I know. And they're going to want me dead whether I'm doing my job or not."

FIVE

Clay watched Summer plead her case with her brother with a little bit of amusement and a lot of observation about both of them that he was mentally filing away. He respected Noah so far—he seemed like a decent guy. And Summer... Clay couldn't get a handle on her. One minute she was friendly. Then next she acted like she couldn't stand his presence.

In either mood, she remained stubborn though, and he couldn't help but admire the trait. Because the stubborn ones tended to be the ones who had the fight to stay alive when it came down to it.

And anyway, he saw something desperate in her eyes, something that told him she'd be better off in the woods, climbing mountains, than trapped inside. He took only a second to decide the extra work it would bring him was worth it, and that the benefits to what she was asking outweighed the risks.

"I think we should let her hike." He winced a little internally at his phrasing. She wasn't going to like the idea that she needed his permission to *let* her hike.

"See, Clay agrees with me." She passed right over it in appreciation for having someone on her side, apparently.

"What's your plan for keeping her safe?"

"I'll be with her, obviously. We'll take my car in case someone is watching hers and hasn't taken note of mine yet, and we'll choose less popular hikes where people aren't going to see her in case the killer is working with a partner."

"Do you think he is?"

"No, I don't. But we need to be as aware as possible. Not cautious in a way that keeps you locked in the lodge till this is figured out, but very aware."

She nodded.

"What do you think?" He directed the question to Noah. Though Clay took his assignment to protect Summer seriously, he knew that Noah's position as her brother, and police chief, meant that he might have stronger opinions and he certainly had the right to them. Clay was just summer help, just a friend, not someone who mattered much in the grand scheme of Summer's life. Even if keeping her safe felt more personal than any job he'd taken before.

"If you're comfortable with it, we'll try it for now."

"Thank you, thank you, thank you." Summer threw her arms around her brother and grinned. She looked back at Clay. "I'll be on my guard. I don't want to make your job any more difficult than it already is."

"Fine. Work it out and call me as soon as you're back at the lodge," Noah said.

Summer nodded.

"We'd better get back inside for now. The fewer people out here in the parking lot, the less chance that one of the guests' attention will be drawn to the vandalism." Clay didn't want to point out the possible implications for their business when Summer's life was so much more important, but the welfare of the lodge seemed important to Summer.

"Right. Thank you." Surprise was in her eyes as she turned to him.

Clay offered a small smile. "So what was wrong earlier?"

"When?"

He studied her face. Shook his head. "Never mind." Whatever the reason for her odd behavior, it seemed to be over now and Clay was only overly curious when it benefitted a case. Otherwise he believed in letting people have their privacy. Their secrets.

He wasn't much of a secret keeper himself. Or he hadn't been, until recently. Now there were parts of himself he didn't have any desire to share with anyone else—thoughts that haunted him when he tried to fall asleep at night.

"Where are you planning to hike today?"

"Bear Creek Falls."

Clay raised his eyebrows. "Bear Creek? Really?"

"Yes, bears. As in those creatures in the woods up here. Why?" The smile that tugged at the edges of her lips showed a hint of amusement. Clay knew he was what Alaskans would occasionally refer to as a cheechako— basically a newbie, unfamiliar with the area—but he'd done a little research on the dangers he could expect to face before coming to Alaska.

"You carry bear spray when you lead these hikes, right?"

Summer rolled her eyes. "I'm from Moose Haven, Alaska, Clay. I carry a .44."

He laughed, something he hadn't been doing enough of lately. "Noted."

"Although I carry spray too. It works out better for everyone if you can deter a bear from attacking with the spray."

Clay nodded. He had both lines of defense Summer had mentioned also, and had planned to wear one on either side of his belt. Better safe than sorry. While the killer after Summer posed a bigger threat, it would be foolish to ignore the wildlife threat on the Kenai Peninsula.

"And this place is not somewhere you regularly hike, correct?" he confirmed as they headed into the lodge. Summer was walking toward the living room.

"That's right. It's been years since I've been there at all." She frowned a little. "I wish I could use my usual places. I have my list of hike routes carefully thought out and edited to include what I think will challenge tourists just enough but still provide a payoff in views or something else. Anything not on that list, there's a reason why it's not ideal for tourists."

"That matters less than keeping you safe."

"True. But I don't think you understand how much my family's lodge means to me."

"Why is that?"

She shifted in her seat. Clay waited, observing the tell and knowing she was either planning to lie—something that didn't seem like her—or avoid telling him the whole truth.

"It's my family's lodge. Why wouldn't I care about it?"

"It just seems to mean even more to you than that."

"Let's focus on the hike, okay?" She opened a drawer in the small end table beside the couch and pulled out a map.

"I should probably get a couple of those while I'm up here so I can learn my way around."

"You'll figure it out quickly enough, at least where roads are concerned. There aren't that many of them. It might take a little longer to get the trails down. Even I don't know where all of those go, which is why I was in trouble the other day."

"What happened that you ended up somewhere you didn't realize where you were?" Clay asked, realizing he didn't think he'd heard that part of the story.

"I had to run from him when I had the chance. He was standing between me and one route I knew, and another route would have meant backtracking down a wide-open trail that would have made it easy for him to follow. I figured the smaller, less used trail was my best bet because I grew up hiking these mountains, dodging trees, running over roots."

"You took a risk and it paid off."

"A calculated one, but yes."

He nodded. "Impressive," he told her truthfully. He wasn't sure Summer understood how remarkable her whole handling of that situation had been.

She shrugged. "I did what I had to do. I still keep re-playing it in my mind. First, in case there are any details I missed that might help and, second, because I wonder what I could have done differently. Could I have avoided it? Should I have reacted in a different way than I did? Things like that." Summer exhaled, her shoulders dropping as she did so.

"You did a good job. Trust me. Now show me where we're going today."

She set the map on her lap, paused and shook her head. "Actually, come with me."

She stood and walked to the stairs, and Clay followed her to the second floor and into her room. "What's up?"

"I just had a bad feeling. I'm probably just jumpy from talking about the attack, but I didn't want to risk being overheard by anyone. If we are supposed to keep the location a secret until we're heading on the hike, to minimize the chances my attacker can find me, that includes keeping it from *everybody* who isn't family. Or you. Or Erynn."

"You don't think there's a connection between your attacker and one of the guests, do you?" The idea had crossed Clay's mind but he'd written it off fairly quickly. If one of the guests wanted Summer dead there would have been plenty of opportunity to attack her closer to the lodge. Following her up the steep mountain trail would have been unnecessary.

"I don't know. I just don't want to take chances."

"Just calculated risks, right?" Clay smiled a little. Whether she acknowledged it or not, Summer was a risk taker. She just had her own unique ideas about what constituted a risk and what didn't.

"So have a seat." She motioned to the two chairs on one wall of the room. Clay sat, Summer taking the seat next to him. She unfolded the map again. "We're here." She set her finger down. Clay nodded, doing his best to memorize the general topography around the lodge, looking for landmarks. "And we're going here."

"Is it a pretty steep hike?"

"Not as steep as the trail I was on yesterday."

"Yeah, but you were on your way up a mountain."

"That's where I prefer to be."

Summer stopped, almost cutting herself off in the middle of the last word. She gazed up at him, her face giving nothing away, but looking like she was studying him, waiting to see if he'd caught something.

"What is it?"

She shook her head. "Nothing."

"I'd already figured out the mountains are home for you, Summer. It's not a secret."

She flinched a little at the word *secret* unless Clay was mistaken.

"So what will you tell people about the hike, as far as difficulty level? I'm guessing you're planning to advertise it in some way so people will know what they're getting into, right?"

Summer exhaled, the tension lines in her face easing. One of these days Clay's curiosity was going to get the best of him—she'd react to something he said, and he wouldn't be able to let it go—but for now it seemed like the right thing to do. Even if Summer was becoming more and more intriguing to him.

"I'll probably call it moderate. A young kid who's a good hiker could do it. I have a friend in Anchorage whose son climbed one of the peaks up here—they call it Little O'Malley—when he was four."

"I'd probably try that one if a four-year-old could do it." Clay laughed.

"I didn't say it was easy. I said a good hiker could handle it. Hiking is less about age or agility and more about your mental state, and how badly you want to be on top of that mountain."

"You think so, huh?"

She nodded, and Clay could tell that once again they were dangerously close to an area of Summer's life that meant enough to her that she guarded it from other people. So there was something about the mountains that was crucially important to her. Interesting.

"What time should we leave on the hike?" she interjected as Clay reminded himself not to push her for answers about things like this, that intrigued him but didn't have anything to do with the case.

"When do you usually schedule them?"

"Sometimes morning, sometimes afternoon. It's just after eight now. We could easily post a 10:30 departure time and take lunch with us, or we could eat here and hike afterward."

"Let's do that, then."

"Thanks for doing this, Clay."

He nodded, smiled back at her and tried not to second-guess everything as she stood up to get ready for the day. He only hoped he was doing the right thing, and not taking risks that would put her in greater danger.

SIX

Hours later, Summer walked along the path to the start of the trail, trying to project the confidence she usually felt. She wasn't sure she was fooling anyone with her attempts not to be scared out of her mind by the fact that someone was after her, but she sure was trying.

Not that she wanted to deceive anyone, but she didn't want to be babied. And most of all, she didn't want anyone blaming her, in any way more than they already legitimately could, for the failure of Moose Haven Lodge.

Summer had no idea why Clay didn't understand how much the lodge meant to her. He had no idea of the circumstances of her past few years, true. So he didn't know that if it weren't for her, the lodge would be sitting pretty, bringing in more than enough money to support all of them. But she'd left right when they needed her most and now things were tight. Most of that weight was on Tyler's shoulders, but Summer didn't want him to have to shoulder that alone.

Besides, whether Clay understood or not, it was her family's lodge and family mattered, so it was her responsibility too. Did Clay not understand that? Maybe not.

She didn't know enough about him. Didn't know if he

even *had* a family. She shuddered at the very thought of being alone in the world. She didn't know what she'd do without her family. They had never let her down...even if she hadn't been able to return the favor.

Pushing the past from her mind, something she felt like she spent too large a portion of every day doing, Summer stared down at her favorite hiking boots. They were covered in dirt, now not just from enjoyable adventures in the woods, not just a visible symbol of how she loved to push herself, but also from running for her life.

Summer wasn't sure how she felt about that. It seemed wrong, somehow. Another thing her mystery attacker had tainted. Nothing about this situation seemed right though. Right down to the fact that as protective as Noah was, her brother didn't have the time to invest in keeping her safe one-on-one, not if he was going to make any headway in solving the case and making something like a protective detail unnecessary.

So she had a stranger keeping her safe.

That was something she needed to get over sooner rather than later. The way she'd behaved toward Clay wasn't something she was proud of and it needed to change.

Summer took a deep breath at the trailhead as she eyed the woods. "'Lovely, dark and deep,'" she muttered under her breath, reminded of a poem she'd studied in high school.

"Robert Frost, right?"

She jumped, not having realized Clay was right behind her. She nodded. "I think so. You read a lot of poetry?" She wouldn't be surprised if he said yes. There was more to him than she would have assumed.

"Not since high school English—I think that's when I read that poem."

She laughed. "Me too."

"It must be required across the country or something."

Summer nodded, having forgotten in the seconds of kinship there that they came from different ends of the country, different worlds if you thought about it. This corner of Alaska was familiar to her, where she was raised—the mountains that were her home. She'd looked Clay up online and learned that he was from South Georgia, near the beach. They couldn't be more opposite if they tried.

"You nervous about going back in the woods?"

The perception she'd noted as being part of his character seemed to be coming out even stronger now. But she didn't see a need to answer. He could take that however he wanted to.

"Alright," she said, raising her voice to be heard by the small crowd, "if everyone will meet me here by the trailhead I need to go over some rules."

She went through her spiel the way she did before every single hike she led—some tourists underestimated the terrain or Alaska itself, and she liked to make sure they understood the risks as well as how to minimize them before they started. Among other things, she reminded them of how to act during a bear encounter and to make sure they stayed with a hiking partner.

"Does this mean you're my hiking partner?" Clay drawled softly as she walked by.

Summer whirled and caught the smile in his eyes. This playfulness was a new side of him. She smiled back for a split second, welcoming the more lighthearted interaction, before realizing she really couldn't afford to let her guard down. For the sake of her safety and her heart. "I guess you don't have much choice right now, do you?"

Not waiting for a reply, Summer started down the trail. Of course, a quick glance over her shoulder not many seconds later, which she told herself was to check on the hikers she was leading, confirmed that he'd caught up and was directly behind her. From the little she knew about him, she was certain he wasn't going to let her go far from him. He took keeping her safe seriously, something she appreciated.

"On the right in just a few more minutes you'll get your first glimpse of the falls," she called back to the group. "We won't reach the base of the falls for another two miles because of the way the trail twists and turns through the forest."

Some appreciative murmurs behind her from the tourists confirmed to Summer that she'd made a good decision for this hike. Of course, it wasn't long after that that she remembered why it wasn't one of her favorite trails—the mud could get slick on some of the uphill sections.

She made it up one particularly steep section and then turned to the group. They seemed to be doing okay so far. She saw more smiles than frowns—so far this hike was a win. She felt her shoulders relax a little as she prepared to deliver her next fun fact about this trail. That was something that made her hikes more enjoyable than people just wandering through the woods by themselves. She was able to offer tourists her expertise about the area and help them recognize some of the unique elements they were seeing.

"I'm sure you're noticing the mud helping you break your hiking boots in." Summer kept her voice light. "For those of you who don't already know, both Moose Haven and the nearby town of Seward are in the farthest north rain forest. I know when you think *rain forest* you probably don't picture spruce trees but it's true."

"Explains the mud," Clay muttered under his breath. Summer glanced at him, catching his smile. He did have a nice smile. More than nice.

They kept hiking.

"Just about another mile to the falls."

Most of the people had stopped talking by now. This was the most intense part of the hike. Thankfully the wind had shifted, bringing some of the cool moist air from the falls their way. Summer brushed her hair from her face as she hiked, noting in amusement how the hairs by her forehead had curled up in the forest's humidity.

A quarter mile from the falls, Clay's demeanor changed. He moved closer to her, keeping in step with her perfectly, walking beside her now, not behind her like he had been earlier.

"What is it?" Summer didn't think anything the man did was without intention.

"I'm not sure yet."

Cryptic, but she was working, she didn't have time to crack his evasive-man code right now.

"Alright, up ahead you'll see Bear Creek Falls." Summer glanced at Clay, who was looking elsewhere, back in the direction they'd come maybe. What did he see back there? She intended to find out, once she'd gotten the tourists settled.

"Please finish making your way to the falls, take some pictures and enjoy—" she glanced at her watch "—forty-five minutes on your own before meeting back here." She motioned to a large spruce tree with a rock underneath it. "Remember, this is the Alaskan wilderness, so be cautious. Yes, there are trails and if it weren't safe in this area, then I wouldn't have brought you here, but you still need to stay alert and pay attention to your surroundings. Make notes of landmarks if you want to wander at all and keep an eye on the clock. I've given the lodge our approximate return time so someone will be coming to check on us if we aren't back when we should be."

Summer stayed still while the group wandered toward the falls, making their way at a leisurely pace down the trail.

When the last tourist had passed her, she turned to Clay. "What is it?"

"I told you I'm not sure yet."

"But you suspect something."

His face was serious, his eyes giving away nothing. He was 100 percent in police officer mode, Summer knew.

"You found something, didn't you? We have some time. Take me with you and let's see what it is."

He shook his head. "I'm not sure you want to be there."

"So what, you're going to take me back down to the lodge, find someone to cover bodyguard duty and come back up here? It would take hours—whatever you thought you saw could be long gone. Plus, you don't know the trail. And anyway, I thought keeping me safe was your job."

Summer was right about one thing. His primary job was keeping her safe. Not just from physical danger, but from anything that would add to her nightmares.

The smell of decaying flesh wasn't something you easily forgot once you'd smelled it, and Clay had before. He'd caught the first whiff on this trail about five minutes back from where they were right now and hadn't decided how he was going to go investigate.

He didn't want Summer to see what he suspected he would find. But he knew that there was no way to stop her from coming with him. And she was right that it made more sense not to wait until later. The faster they confirmed his suspicions, the faster they could notify the authorities and get a proper investigation started. He started walking back along the trail, and Summer followed him.

"Remind me how far this trail is from where you were attacked."

Summer shrugged. "It depends. It would take probably about four hours following the twists and turns on the trail from where we are now, give or a take a little time, unless someone took the ridgeline." She motioned upward. Clay wasn't sure where they were on this mountain.

"How close are we to the top?"

"Not quite two-thirds of the way up. This is the last of the tree line. Another quarter mile or so and it's clear mountain."

"Have you done the ridgeline, then?" Clay suspected he knew the answer but wanted to hear it from Summer.

She nodded. "Yes."

"Were you planning to do it the other night?"

She exhaled. "No."

"No?"

She shook her head.

"Is it possible that someone could have attacked you over on Hope Mountain and then come over here by the ridgeline, or vice versa?"

"Sure, but I don't know why it would matter."

Clay picked up his pace and Summer followed. "What is that smell?"

It was getting stronger the closer they backtracked to where Clay had first smelled it. The wind had shifted again, which apparently was causing Summer to notice it too.

"We'll see in a minute," he said with no hint of amusement in his voice.

Clay paused and motioned to the left. "Is there a trail that will get us that way?"

"Besides the ridgeline?"

Her voice still had a hint of teasing—she must not recognize the smell.

"I need a trail that goes that way, Summer."

She seemed to finally recognize that he didn't have any room for humor at the moment.

She studied the direction he'd pointed and seemed to finally find a way that would work. "Game trail. This way."

She stepped in front of him but Clay caught her arm. Summer paused, then looked at his hand on her arm.

Clay released it immediately, breaking the touch. She'd been attacked just hours before, what had he been thinking?

He hadn't been thinking at all—he'd been reacting on instinct. And he'd learned the hard way that his instincts couldn't always be trusted.

"I'm so sorry."

"It was fine, actually." She was still studying her arm, where his hand had been. She looked up slowly, met his eyes and held her gaze there. "It wasn't the same at all, the way you touched me. I could tell your intention was to keep me safe."

She exhaled. Relieved to know her attack hadn't scarred her more than it could have, maybe? Clay knew she was fortunate to have escaped more mental trauma. Some people weren't so fortunate.

"I need to go first." Clay focused back on the task at hand.

"Why?"

"Summer." He didn't seem to have more words than that, couldn't find any in his mind. They hiked in silence for a minute. Then Summer spoke up again.

"Why won't you tell me what we're looking for?" Summer coughed. "And what *is* that smell?" She looked around.

And saw it a split second before Clay did, if the way she stilled was to be believed. She inhaled sharply, but didn't look away. Neither did Clay, because that was what he'd been searching for.

The source of the smell. Fifteen or twenty yards away.

Female. Midtwenties.

Blonde.

This was a match for the serial killer's MO after all, which meant the case had turned from bad to worse. Their worst nightmare for keeping Summer safe seemed to be coming true.

Clay had called the Moose Haven Police Department to report the discovery of the body as soon as he saw it. Summer, seeing they were going to have to wait there for a while until law enforcement showed up to secure the scene, called Kate, who agreed to hike up to Bear Creek Falls to meet the group and lead them back to the lodge. The group of tourists wasn't going to be told about the body, though if it ended up in the paper they'd make the connection eventually. For now, it was better they not know.

Now they were waiting, one of the worst parts when something like this happened. In the movies, once a body was discovered or a crime was committed, everything sped up, but real life didn't work that way. The Moose Haven PD was sending officers but it would take them a while to arrive at the scene and then it would have to be processed, with a methodicalness that wouldn't allow them to rush at all, needing to see if there were any clues the killer had left behind.

"Do you know who the victim could be?" He hated to ask but needed to. The police would want to know and it helped him think through the implications of finding a body in the woods also. Besides, it gave him a reason to try to keep Summer looking at him, rather than at the body lying there on the forest floor not too far from them.

Not that either of them could forget it was there.

Summer started to shake her head and then paused. "Possibly. Someone mentioned this morning on a hiking page I follow online that a friend was missing. It didn't jump out at me because that's fairly common up here. When someone goes missing it's rarely foul play, at least among missing persons cases I've heard of."

"Tell me about the person who was missing. Do you remember anything specific about her?"

"Basically what you can see." She winced. "Just that she was around my age… That she was an avid hiker and adventurer. She did some hiking videos telling people about the hikes she liked to do. Those are online somewhere."

Clay's heartbeat quickened. "Did she post ahead of

time what hikes she'd be talking about next?" That could have given their killer a way to find her. He'd been wondering how the man had managed to track two women on mountains next to each other at the same time unless he'd known where they both were going to be ahead of time. They'd already established that Summer's routine was set enough he'd probably been able to know exactly where she'd be, but this woman's death and the circumstances around it were still a mystery.

Clay's gut said that once they cracked the mystery, the answers would bring them a step closer to whoever was after Summer.

But that hadn't happened yet, he reminded himself. He needed that investigative team to hurry up and get here.

"I think she did, yes," Summer answered his question, nodding slowly like she'd realized why he'd asked it and was putting the pieces together for herself.

"And someone could hike that ridgeline."

"Only someone experienced. It's not a ridgeline I could see a novice doing with any success."

He pressed for more details. "How experienced?"

"Intermediate."

"Okay." So it wouldn't narrow their suspect list solely to expert mountain climbers, but at least it gave them a direction to look in.

Movement down the trail caught his attention. His hand immediately went to his side, the familiar bulk of his service handgun there and ready if he needed it. Thankfully he spotted Noah and a female state trooper officer coming up the trail. He moved his hand off his weapon and called to them.

Noah's face registered the exact moment he smelled

the distinct odor of decay. He felt for the police chief. Clay had kept himself and Summer there not only because the body needed to be kept under supervision until the law enforcement could come to process it, but also because he'd learned in his years of police work that the best course of action was to stay at the scene and let your nose get used to the smell. It was better than getting fresh air and coming back in, a mistake rookie cops often made. It usually didn't take them long to learn though.

"Tell me how you found her." Noah's voice was all business, the strain of the day already evident in his tone, and Clay knew it was only going to get worse.

"The smell first. Then I came this way to investigate."

"Did it occur to you that you were marching my sister into a crime scene?" Noah practically growled the words.

"Noah. Calm down. He did what needed to be done." The trooper stuck her hand out to Clay. "Trooper Erynn Cooper."

"Trooper...Cooper?"

She rolled her eyes. "Yeah, never heard that before. Clever."

Clay smiled. "Sorry, ma'am."

"Ma'am?" Now her brows were raised. The woman had a really expressive face. "Where are you from, because it's sure not here."

"Georgia."

"The South. That makes sense."

"Could we save the introductions for later?"

Erynn rolled her eyes and gave Clay a sympathetic smile. "He's really not always such a bear."

Clay looked between the two of them. "Do the troopers work with Moose Haven police often?"

Erynn nodded as Noah shook his head.

Summer sighed. "They have to cooperate because Moose Haven is in such an isolated area of the Kenai Peninsula. Because of that our police force is small and sometimes needs backup." She nodded to Erynn. "And sometimes the troopers need Moose Haven PD's help with particular cases because they technically have jurisdiction and the troopers don't like to supersede that when they don't need to." She nodded at Noah. "Did I balance that well between the two of you so we can give up the fighting for now?"

Noah glared.

"So." Erynn moved closer to the body. "I think this is our missing person from Kenai. The hiking blogger— Melissa Mitchell."

Noah stepped closer to see as well, and then looked back at Clay. Clay knew what the other man was about to ask. It was time for Summer to get out of there. Pretty soon reality was going to hit, the knowledge that she could have ended up just like that, how close she'd come to being a body in the woods.

It roiled Clay's stomach, and without thinking he reached out his left hand. Somehow he just needed physical contact with her right now as they made their way through the growing dimness of this thick area of forest. It was still early enough for plenty of daylight but the clouds had darkened, another heavy rain promising to be released soon in the future.

If she was surprised at his gesture, she didn't show it. Just accepted his offered hand. It took him off guard how much smaller her hand was than his. So feminine and soft. He guessed he hadn't spent much time thinking about what her hands were like, but for someone who was so tough and independent, she was also so fragile.

Clay couldn't let anything happen to her.

"Let's go," he said to her.

"You don't have to ask me again."

SEVEN

Summer couldn't quite get comfortable anywhere at the lodge, not after what they'd found that afternoon. Clay had been quieter than usual since they'd returned and the several attempts at conversation she'd made had been unsuccessful.

She'd finally given up and sat down with a sketchbook and some charcoal pencils. Her family teased her about how rarely she sat still, so this old hobby wasn't one she had much time for anymore, but she did enjoy it when she got the chance.

"You're very good." Clay sat down beside her on the couch, leaning over slightly, she guessed to see what she was working on.

"Thanks." She tilted the pad toward him. "Bear Creek Falls. I wanted to remember what the falls themselves look like, remind myself right now that I like that trail, it's a good spot in the woods and it's not the mountain's fault that…" She couldn't make herself finish.

Everything that had happened was settling into her mind, and she knew it was changing the way she viewed the world. Darkening it. Even the lodge that had been her home since she could remember wasn't the same.

That was why she hadn't been able to get comfortable. Somehow everything had changed for Summer since the body had been discovered.

Because it wasn't *a body*. It was a woman who'd been living, moving, warm flesh and blood like she was right now.

And the person who wanted Summer dead might be the same person who'd taken that other life.

It could have been her.

It almost *was* her.

"I see why you'd want to draw it. Got any others in that book?"

She didn't know how much to show him. Was he humoring her, or was he really curious? Then again, did it really matter? He was offering them both something to distract them from the case and the overwhelming feeling that when Noah got home any minute, the news he brought with him might crush her beyond what she could bear.

"A few." She kept her voice calm and handed the book to him. It might be easier if she just let him look rather than be involved in showing him.

He took the sketchbook, started at the beginning, something she admired about him. Any artist's work, in Summer's opinion, should be viewed not only as individual pieces but as a series, because that's how people were—a series of things that happened to them, ways they'd changed, different characteristics…

"These are amazing, Summer."

It only took him a minute or two to flip through them all slowly. She thought she might be up to sketch number eight in this book. Not much compared to the hundred or so pages waiting to be filled. But it had been a long time since she'd slowed down, or *been* slowed down enough to pick the hobby up again.

"Thank you." She never knew what else to say when someone complimented something she enjoyed that came so easily to her.

"It's easy to see that you love the mountains. How long have you been hiking seriously?"

"Hiking? Since I was a kid." She could ignore his "seriously," right? Maybe he hadn't meant it the way she would have naturally interpreted it.

"Not just hiking in general, but like you do now. You hike like an athlete, like it's something you've trained for."

Were *all* cops this observant?

"Since I was seventeen." The words tumbled out before she could question them, and now she couldn't call them back. Summer didn't know how to interpret her current emotions. She was scared, tense, but somehow felt less guarded around Clay than she had. Because of what had happened today, what they'd been through together so far?

She wasn't sure.

The front door of the lodge opened before Clay could ask any follow-up questions, something for which she was thankful since she wasn't sure she was ready for those yet.

"Clay? Summer?"

It was Noah.

"In here," Summer called.

She heard Noah's heavy footsteps approach and studied him as he entered. He looked like he'd aged a couple of years today, and his eyes had growing dark circles underneath them. Had he slept since all this had begun? Summer wasn't sure.

"What did you find out?" she asked before she could stop herself, before she could consider she might not want to know.

"I've got to head back to the station. I'm just here to grab food and check in with you to make sure you're fine."

"She's okay," Clay said. "I'm not letting her out of my sight for longer than it takes to use the bathroom."

"Keep it that way." Noah's voice was nearly vibrating with tension.

"So it's him."

"Him? You found a guy?"

Neither man answered. She understood, gradually. "Ohh. You didn't find anyone. But now you think it's the…serial killer." The last two words she had to force from her mouth, and even as she did she could hardly bring herself to believe this was her real life. That the words *serial killer* had any place in her vocabulary.

Noah exhaled. "I'm almost positive."

"Because we know now that there was a second victim—like his usual pattern?"

Noah hesitated, then nodded. Summer narrowed her eyes. Her brother wasn't lying, but he wasn't telling the whole truth, either.

"What other reason do you have?"

Noah looked at Clay. Neither one of them said anything.

"You've got to stop keeping things from me. It's not making me any safer." Surely they'd respond to that line of argument, since it was such a high priority for both of them.

"Fine." Noah took a breath. "A forensic artist in Anchorage was able to generate a sketch of the suspect based on the description you gave us." He reached into the backpack he'd set on the floor and motioned for them to follow him to the back kitchen, where the family had a private eating area.

They did so. Summer took her seat, trying not to get her hopes up that the sketch was accurate and detailed enough to be useful. She'd have drawn it herself but she didn't draw people, the nuances of facial structure and expression had always eluded her, and though he'd had a mask covering all but his eyes, she'd still feared she wouldn't get it right if she did it herself. But as an artist she knew what an almost impossible proposition it was to draw something based on someone else's description.

Noah set the manila envelope down on the table and opened it.

And there he was, staring at her behind the mask he'd worn. Everything, down to the expression in his eyes, was right. Summer shivered.

"That's him."

Noah nodded. "It also matches the only possible description we had of the serial killer. One of the women who ended up dead, Holly Wilcox, was seen with a man a few hours before her death, walking on one of the multi-use trails in Anchorage. A bicyclist remembered him and gave a description that was, unfortunately, too vague for the artist to work with, as talented as he is. But when I asked him if what he'd drawn for you fit that other man, he thought it did."

"Interesting that she was seen with him and no one noticed a struggle or anything," Clay mused.

"She knew him, then," Summer said. "Right?"

"Possibly."

"And you think he's the man who's killed those other women and is after me." Her mind was refusing to wrap all the way around this new bit of news. Maybe the human mind wasn't made to absorb so much in such a short period of time, because try as she might Summer couldn't quite get herself to acknowledge that this was her reality.

"What else?" she asked, even though she wasn't sure what else she could handle.

The two men looked at each other again, but right before Summer was ready to let her frustration explode again, Clay took her by the arm. "We'll be back," he said to Noah, leading her back farther into the private part of the house and stopping in a hallway where he stood across from her, facing her.

"You've got to stop asking to be told more than you need to know."

"I'm the victim…attempted victim, whatever the correct terminology is." She shoved back a piece of her hair that had fallen in front of her eyes and lifted her chin a little, doing everything she knew how to do to project confidence and certainty, hoping to convince Clay that she was strong enough to handle this.

Clay only shook his head.

"Do you know anything about cases like this, Summer? Do you even have a clue what Noah is dealing with?"

"I don't," she admitted. It was as far from her comfort zone as anything could be. But it *was* happening to her, and Summer was not the kind of woman to back down from a threat, or hide from it. Much as some people might prefer to live with their heads in the sand, that wasn't Summer.

"Everything we saw today was just a glimpse. Do you realize that? There's so much more that will go into the investigation. Autopsies. Analyzing time of death, exact cause of death, whether there was any other trauma… I don't want you to hear those details. And neither does Noah. But even if he did, I'd fight him on this."

"Why? Why do you care so much?"

"Because you're the kind of person who shouldn't have to deal with this."

"I'm not some fragile Southern belle, Clay. I'm an Alaskan woman who has dealt with life and death more than you could probably guess and has faced down both, when they seemed equally scary, and barely flinched."

A slight hint of a smile crossed his face. "First, if you think Southern belles are fragile, you haven't met one. I should introduce you to some of my friends. Second, I'm sorry you've had to do that. I have no doubt you did it well and bravely, but I'm the one in charge of protecting you right now and if I can protect your heart and your mind as well as protect your physical life, I'm going to."

Summer swallowed hard. Her heart was pounding, higher in her throat than it should be from the intensity of this entire conversation. Much as she was worried about her physical life and her mind, it was her heart that had her on shaky ground right now. It was time to stop denying she felt any attraction for Clay Hitchcock. Her only course of action now was to remind herself of all the reasons why it didn't matter, why it would never work.

Because the man had a passion and a caring that wove together into an almost irresistible combination, and Summer couldn't pretend any longer that wasn't true.

But she would protect her heart. She had to. Because she knew what happened when she let her heart get involved—she lost sight of everything but the object of her affection, and last time she'd done that her family had suffered.

She felt the rhythm of her heart beating, enjoyed for just one more second the weight of Clay's hand on her hand and then pulled hers away.

"Keeping me entirely safe is not a job anyone is asking you to do Clay. And it may not be a job you can do."

They rejoined Noah and heard one more update. The crime lab in Anchorage had analyzed the fibers found on Summer's clothes and on the tree branches where the struggle had taken place. They were fleece, and the composition matched the Anchorage Outdoor Gear's store brand. As people from all walks of life shopped there, it still didn't give them much to go on.

Clay would ask Noah what else he had when Summer went to bed tonight. She may not want the kind of sheltering he was trying to give her, but that wasn't going to stop him for now, not when Noah agreed she didn't need to know all the details.

The truth was that this guy was vicious. From a quick conversation when Summer had gone to the bathroom, Clay had learned that the killer was worse than anyone either he or Noah had ever dealt with. The only plus side to anything they'd learned about him today was that with as bold as he was, the risks he took were going to lead law enforcement to catch up to him eventually.

All that troubled him was whether or not that would occur before anything worse happened to Summer.

Time moved slowly. Summer spent some time updating Kate on what had happened. After they all ate a late dinner, Clay suggested a card game to Summer to help pass the time, but the look she gave him more than answered his question about whether or not she was interested in that. Finally he gave up on trying to entertain her and just sat quietly, his mind going over and over the details of the case they knew already and wondering how they'd fill in the ones they didn't. There had to be something more proactive they could do than sit in the lodge, but Clay hadn't figured out what that could be yet.

He glanced at Summer, something telling him he should ask her, but he couldn't quite convince himself to willingly put her through the stress of thinking through the case in deeper detail.

She caught him staring and met his gaze. "What?"

He shook his head. Maybe tomorrow he'd talk to her about it. But he just wasn't sure enough yet that it was a good idea.

"I'm going to bed." She stood. Clay glanced at the clock. Not long past ten but it had been a long day.

"Sleep well." He stood too and started to follow her.

"You don't need to follow me."

He let her walk upstairs alone, but when he heard the door to her room shut, he headed up too and sat down in a chair he'd positioned earlier in the hallway outside her door. He and Noah still hadn't figured out quite what to do about nighttime. Someone needed to be watching Summer at all times, but if the two of them didn't get sleep they wouldn't be any good at providing daytime protection in the long run. Clay had mentioned Tyler as an option, but Noah didn't want his brother adding anything to his plate since he was the one keeping the lodge going while the rest of them focused their energies on this. Clay suspected Noah probably hadn't slept more than three or four hours since all this had started. The man wore a double weight—he was her brother and the police chief. Clay didn't have that pressure…

Instead the pressure he felt came from inside. He cared about Summer not because of anything he *was* to her. He was her friend, and barely that. But he still cared. He chose not to examine the reasons why.

EIGHT

Summer lay in bed staring at the ceiling for what felt like hours, turning one way, then another. A serial killer was after her. She was being protected by a man who threatened the security of the walls she'd been building around her heart for years. Her brother had morphed from his lighthearted self into 100 percent police chief mode. Stress had always made Noah more driven, but Summer never would have guessed the intensity a threat against one of his siblings would bring out.

For the first time, Summer felt like she understood a little more why her siblings had reacted about Christopher the way they had. She'd always seen herself as sort of the extra sibling. Noah was saving the world; Tyler had always wanted to save the lodge; Kate was strong enough to never need saving by anyone but God.

And then there was Summer. The dreamer. The one who made mistakes and needed to be rescued.

She was tired of playing that part. She was going to help with this case, was going to be the one to solve it even, maybe. She was determined, and had already thought of some ideas for how she could contribute to the investigation—she just needed to get Clay on her side. She'd seen in his eyes though his dislike of being on the sidelines, so she should be able to convince him.

She exhaled, exhaustion finally creeping toward her, sleep begging her to close her eyes. She gave in, nodded off slowly and surrendered to unconsciousness.

Her eyes stayed closed when a hand gently stroked her cheek the first time. The second time she blinked her eyes open, confusion muddling with tiredness in her mind. She should be the only one in her room…

As her eyes focused on the black mask in front of her, the man leaning over her bed inches from her face, she almost couldn't breathe. Her nightmare there, in her room. While she slept.

She hadn't even opened her mouth to scream before he put a gloved hand over it. The gloves weren't rough, a detail her mind somehow noticed. They weren't soft, either. They were…squishy. Almost like neoprene?

Summer took note of the detail, even though she didn't know what difference it made. She wasn't trained for what to notice in situations like this and wasn't sure she'd make it out of it anyway.

No, that was no way to think. She refused to keep thinking like a victim, refused to be one. She'd spent too many years of her life living that way, as a self-inflicted victim of her own bad choices. She wasn't going to be anyone's victim now.

She bit down hard on the hand over her mouth, causing the intruder to cry out.

Rather than release her though, he gripped her arm with his other hand even tighter. Summer shivered, not just from his touch, and her eyes went to the window. Open.

At least she'd figured out how he'd gotten in the room.

The handle of her door moved.

Another intruder? The serial killer worked alone, didn't he? Or could the person at her door be help? She fought a wave of dizziness after thinking of the man holding her as not just "her attacker" but "the serial killer." She had been pinned down, and was now being hauled to the window by the hands of a man who had brutally murdered seven women.

"Are you okay in there?" Clay's voice. *He* was the one at the door. She could have cried, if she could get herself to feel anything but terror in the deepest core of her being. All the other emotions seemed dormant. Yet his voice still reminded her to struggle, to make it as difficult as possible for the man trying to haul her away.

"Stop fighting me. This is for your own good." Her captor moved her toward the window another step.

"I'm coming in, so if you aren't decent, now would be a good time to grab a robe or something." Clay's voice was low and serious, heavy with fear that mirrored exactly how she felt. Had he heard the man when she bit him?

"Summer. Now. We have to leave before they stop us." The killer was insistent.

And he knew her name. Summer shivered. It was something that made sense, but it eliminated any possibility that this could be random. And it might mean something to the investigators that he knew it, called her by it. Summer didn't know, didn't know much of anything anymore.

She swallowed hard, tears finally finding their way to her eyes and threatening to spill over. She blinked them back. No, she wouldn't give him the satisfaction of seeing her as anything even approaching weak.

She shook her head and pulled against him. The pressure on her arm increased as he squeezed her. She fought back, twisted away, but he held tight.

The door slammed open.

"Freeze!" Clay yelled.

Summer fell to the ground instantly as the man released her. She took a deep breath. It was almost over.

But her attacker was through the window before Clay had even made it past the bed.

There was a shuffling in the hallway. Before Summer could look up from where she'd crumpled on the floor, Clay addressed him.

"Noah, he's running."

Then more footsteps as her brother took off, presumably out of the house to chase whoever was responsible. It wasn't over yet. And if he could get this close and they still couldn't catch him... A small sob escaped.

Clay bent down, sat on the floor beside her. "Are you okay?"

He asked it slowly, somehow the sound of his low voice putting her more at ease. She shook her head. Paused, then nodded. "I'm okay. Scared. But not injured. Not broken."

She looked up from the floor, where she'd been staring, processing, trying to get ahold of herself now that adrenaline had faded and her hands had started shaking a bit.

"I can't believe I just sat out there in the hallway while he was in here. That he got to you on my watch..." Clay shook his head, then took a deep breath that was long enough for Summer to tell he was having a hard time getting ahold of his emotions too. "I'm sorry, Summer."

Hearing his voice say her name erased some of the

tension in her shoulders. He was helping the whole experience lose its power, being here with her like this. She reached a hand over to him, knowing he wouldn't misinterpret it as a romantic gesture, but just as her needing reassurance that someone was there. That she was okay.

He took her hand. Slowly ran his thumb across it and tightened his grip ever so slightly.

"You did the best you could," she offered, wanting him to stop blaming himself.

"No. And I need to let you help."

Leaving her hand in the warmth of his, she looked up at him. "What?"

"Sitting around waiting for him to attack is crazy. We have to do something."

He was so closely echoing her own thoughts from earlier. Summer nodded. "I have an idea."

Before she could tell him, Noah burst back into the room.

"Did you get him?"

"He's gone." Noah shook his head. "Vanished completely, as if he knew of some hidden trail even though I've lived here on this property my whole life. I looked for tracks and I've got Kate out there now, with one of my officers, looking in case I missed anything."

Summer respected the fact that her brother wasn't embarrassed to admit that Kate was the better tracker of the two of them. She was one of the best trackers in all of Alaska, which was saying something. Summer couldn't read signs like she could, but she could find her way around in the woods with ease, which was why her being disoriented after the attack and not recognizing where she was had cut so deep and disconcerted her so much.

"He can't just have disappeared."

Noah shook his head. "I'll stay with Summer if you want to investigate."

Summer watched the two of them stare each other down. There seemed to be something going on that she wasn't aware of, some sort of unspoken conversation happening between the two of them.

Feeling frustrated that she was once again being left out of the loop, she tried to think of a way she could help. "Listen, I can go check myself if you want."

"You won't be leaving the house until it's time for you to go to a safe house, which is as soon as I get a place cleared and set up." Noah's voice didn't leave any room for argument.

Didn't faze Summer.

"I'm not going to a safe house."

"We'll talk about it later."

She shook her head. "No. Not unless you can be absolutely certain I'd be any safer there." Besides, even if running and hiding did appeal to some cowardly place inside her, not only did Summer refuse to give in to that, she also needed to be here at the lodge. Her hikes were usually some of the best-rated amenities the lodge offered. It wasn't so much that she did anything that was so different from anyone they could have hired to lead the hikes, but rather because she was something of a minor celebrity in athletic circles. If people were fascinated by her mountain running credentials and the brief note in her bio about the time she'd spent in Europe running with some of the world's elite on some of the most stunning peaks on the globe, then that was fine with her—as long as it brought more business to the lodge. It meant she was finally doing something for her family, contributing.

Atoning.

"I'm not leaving." Her voice was just as firm.

Noah exhaled. "Fine. I'll leave it for the moment. For now, get dressed." He looked at Clay. "Someone else will cover your assigned tasks at the lodge for both of you today. You need to go to Anchorage to talk to some of the officers who have been working this case. I've communicated to them everything you've told me, but maybe a face-to-face will help and they'll uncover something that will point us to our target. We need a break in this case. This guy is too good."

Clay was nodding. "I'd been thinking we should go up there."

Summer's heartbeat quickened. She'd been planning a trip to Alaska's largest city also, but for slightly different case-related reasons. "Alright, when do we leave?"

Noah raised his eyebrows. Surprised by her easy acquiescence? She wasn't sure. But she didn't flinch, didn't lower her shoulders.

"As soon as you're ready," Clay answered.

She glanced at the clock. It was 3:52 a.m. She wasn't going back to sleep. "Give me five minutes."

"We might need to stay in Anchorage through tomorrow." Summer waited till they were well down the Seward Highway headed toward Anchorage before she started sharing the pieces of her plan with Clay. They were out of cell phone signal range right now, so she knew he couldn't call Noah to get his thoughts on it, a detail that may or may not have factored into her decision to broach the subject right now.

"Why is that?" Clay looked over at her, only briefly as he put his eyes right back on the road, but it was long enough for her to wonder about the thoughts behind what she saw in his eyes. He'd weathered the situation well, showing up in town right as everything in her family went crazy and jumping right in to help. She remembered Tyler talking about him from college but hadn't realized they were that close—close enough for Clay to put himself in danger to protect Tyler's family.

Or maybe Clay was just like that. That wouldn't surprise her. He seemed like the kind of classic Southern boy who would pull his friends' trucks out of ditches in the middle of the night, no questions asked, like the kind you heard about in songs. Until now she hadn't been sure they actually existed. Alaskans had their own code of honor, committed to taking care of their own, but it still wasn't the same as whatever she saw in Clay.

She wondered how much of it had to do with his faith. She'd seen him reading his Bible on more than one occasion when they'd been sitting in the lodge. Really reading, like he was paying attention too, not just holding it and staring into the distance like she'd done the last few times she'd tried it.

Before she'd acknowledged that maybe, possibly, it was too late for her.

She shrugged the uncomfortable thoughts away before they could settle too deeply in her mind. "Because I have a plan."

"Go on."

His voice was cautious. Hesitant, but not necessarily filled with any kind of opposition. Not yet anyway.

"After we talk to the police, I want to talk to some of the victims' families."

"The police will have handled that, Summer. And I'm not sure they'll give us access to that—though it's likely something Noah can get ahold of if he feels like he should."

"Hear me out."

Another glance. Some crazy part of her wanted to reach out her hand, hold his again like she had in the early hours of this morning and see if the same electricity shot through her, the heart-shaking, unsettling but so-very-welcome kind.

Welcome?

No. That kind of heat was dangerous. Lack of sleep and extremely close proximity to Clay were just getting to her, that was all. People had all kinds of weird emotions when they were stuck with someone in these kinds of emotional, tense situations.

She shook her head, focusing on what she'd been saying. "I just need to talk to them myself and ask some questions I don't think the police would have asked."

"The police are good at what they do. And they won't release any additional information on the victims or their families. I'm sorry, I'm trying to hear you out, Summer, but none of this sounds like anything I can help you with."

"I've got a list of names and addresses," she said before he could say anything else.

"How?"

Summer shrugged. "I read the news articles, did some digging online, as much as I could."

Clay didn't say anything for a minute. Summer looked out the window as they started gaining elevation, moving into Turnagain Pass, the last bit of isolated highway before they started edging closer toward the limits of the Municipality of Anchorage.

"Why?"

"Think about it, Clay. I'm being targeted. I must have something in common with these women, or he wouldn't have gone after all of us. I'm one of them, but…not."

"And you won't be if I have anything to say about it."

He practically growled the words, but in a protective way. She almost smiled, but Summer had more to say, so she kept going. "Are you going to listen to the rest?"

"I'm sorry, go ahead."

"Thank you. I think it's more than just a physical description connection. There must at the very least be some way he knew all of us, or had seen all of us… something that drew us to his attention. Right? Surely he didn't just drive down to the Moose Haven area of all places and stalk the first two people he met who looked like the other women he'd killed?" Summer wasn't sure, she could be reaching there, but she knew if she was Clay would tell her. To be honest, she wasn't sure if her speculation had her on the right track or not, but sitting around waiting for someone to try to kill her again wasn't working for her. She had to do something, be involved somehow, and this was the best way she could think of. Besides, it made sense to her, that maybe this could help them make progress. If there was even a chance, it was worth it to her to try.

"It's a reasonable question to be asking."

"So if he knew all of us, maybe I'll be able to figure out a connection if I can talk personally to the families."

"They may not let you, you know."

"The police?"

"No, the families. This is painful for them. They may not want to revisit it, especially with a woman who at least vaguely resembles the person they lost."

"That I understand." Summer hesitated. "But if it

would save someone's life? Or maybe more important for them, if it would bring a killer to justice?" Her heart was beating faster now, but for once in the last few days, it wasn't because of fear but anticipation. Somehow she thought this would work.

He reached over, squeezed her hand and let it go before she even knew what was happening.

Blinking, she moved her hand to her lap when he released it—which was almost as soon as he'd touched it, it was that fast—and looked over at him.

Clay smiled. "I think we've got a shot at finding something we can use today. It's a good idea, it really is. I just don't want you to get your hopes up."

She understood that. That was the dangerous thing about hope—when it didn't come through for you, it was almost worse than if you'd never had any in the first place.

Her hand still tingling from Clay's touch, she angled her body a little more toward the window and looked out at the scenery as they drove, ticking off reasons in her head why she shouldn't let herself care that he'd touched her hand.

She was being stalked by a killer. He was only staying for the summer.

And most important, she'd made mistakes and he seemed like the poster child for a Christian nice guy.

Yes, sometimes hope wasn't worth the pain it caused.

NINE

Summer had gone quiet after sharing her plan with him, and while Clay knew his mental energy would be better spent thinking about the case, he couldn't stop thinking about how she was acting.

Was it his fault, because of that quick hand squeeze?

He wasn't the best with women, wasn't one of those guys who charmed his way into a date often. He wouldn't say he couldn't, he'd just rarely tried to be flirtatious because it seemed dishonest to him—if he wanted to get to know a woman better, he'd be straightforward.

Not that he'd been trying to do that with Summer. Nothing like that had been on his mind. Only a strong admiration for how quick thinking she was, and the desire to show her he was on her side. That he cared.

All it had done was push her away.

It took all Clay's focus to keep driving and not pull over and go for a walk in the woods. Or a run, that would be better. He missed the routine he'd had to keep himself in shape back when he was a police officer. He could easily maintain the same habits now but driving across the country had thrown that schedule off some. He needed to get back into the swing of that. He glanced at Summer. He considered bringing up to her now the idea of them running together—to get him back into shape and to let her get out of the house while still being protected—but from the way she leaned away from him to the way her arms were folded, everything about her said "no trespassing."

Instead he just drove, through the vastness of the Kenai Peninsula, up into Turnagain Pass, then around Turnagain Arm as they approached Anchorage from the south side.

Summer broke the silence. "When we get to the police department, they won't separate us, will they? I mean, we're not suspects so it's not like TV. Right?"

Clay's shoulders relaxed a little at a conversation he could easily handle. "Not at all. They just want to share information, really. They may treat you a bit like—"

"Like a victim?" Her tone made no secret of her hatred for that word. It wasn't something anyone wanted to be, a *victim*, but something about how strongly Summer rebelled against the designation made him wonder if there was more to it in her case, some aspect of her life that he didn't know about. Which wouldn't be difficult as he hadn't known her for a full week yet, though in some ways it felt like he had known her for years.

"Right."

"But you'll be there."

"Yes. I'll make sure they understand we have to stay together. Your brother wouldn't want us separated."

"Just my brother?"

Something about the way she asked it caught his attention—she was not speaking in a coy way at all, her tone was just honest. Like she wanted to know what he thought of her, if he cared. How much of this was a job and how much was because he didn't want to see her hurt.

Clay didn't know. He was afraid to let himself think through any of the possible answers.

"I don't want it, either, Summer. I can keep you safer when I'm with you." He took a deep breath, determined to make up the ground he'd lost with the hand-holding incident. "It's my job." He added the last three words knowing full well he cared more than he would about some random person he felt obliged to protect, which was all Summer had been to him before he had started to get to know her.

"It is. You're right."

She grew quiet again and Clay didn't mind it as much as they entered Anchorage and traffic started to get thicker. They'd hit right about at the morning rush hour, or so it seemed. He wasn't sure how long rush hour lasted there, he only knew that compared to Treasure Point and Moose Haven, the traffic was thick. He got off the highway when they were well into town and, following the directions he'd gotten from the internet, arrived at the Anchorage Police Department.

"Has Anchorage been working on tracking this guy, or would it be better to talk to the troopers?" Summer asked with a frown after Clay pulled into a parking place in front of the building.

"We'll talk to both. They have both worked on the cases here in town."

"So they don't mind sharing information with each other, things like that?"

Clay laughed. "Don't believe everything you see on TV. Most law enforcement departments are perfectly happy to have more manpower working on a case. Gets through evidence faster, prevents some backlogging."

She nodded, but didn't say anything more.

They entered through the front doors and Clay told the receptionist who they were there to see. The detective Noah had told him to ask for came through a security door only a few minutes later. He held it open and motioned for them to enter.

"Clay Hitchcock? Summer Dawson? I'm George Walters. Thank you for coming. We've been hoping to talk to you, but it didn't sound initially like you'd be able to make the trip up from the Kenai. Did your drive go well?"

"No traffic, roads were great," Summer confirmed. "It's nice that the snow is melted now."

"It is. It's tricky getting up here in the winter."

Clay hadn't considered that, but when he thought about it, he realized the Seward Highway, which they'd just taken, was the only road between the whole Kenai Peninsula—not just Moose Haven but also five to ten other medium-sized towns, he'd guess from the maps he'd looked at—and Anchorage.

"If you'll both come to my office." He stopped at a doorway and motioned them inside. Clay stopped to let Summer go first and she did so, and then he followed.

"Thank you again for meeting with us," Clay said as he sat. "We had another incident last night and wanted to make sure everyone working on this case had as many details as possible."

"Chief Dawson told me some of it this morning, though not specifics. I wanted to get those from Miss Dawson firsthand. I appreciate you both making the trip—anything that could help us make some progress."

Walters ran a hand across his forehead as he shook his head. "I don't like knowing this guy is out there somewhere. I don't feel like any of the women in our city are really safe—or apparently the entire area." He looked at Summer.

She didn't say anything but Clay thought she looked a little nervous. He decided he'd better talk first. She could answer questions once Walters asked some.

"Do you guys happen to have any idea why he might have moved onto women on the Kenai?"

Walters seemed to weigh his words. "I understand you're former law enforcement, Clay. So you'll understand why I can't answer that question fully. Here's what I know. We're working with a profiler at the FBI to try to figure out his motives, try to decipher if his MO might change. The move to another location surprised the guys at the FBI and us too, but there are possible explanations."

Clay nodded. He could respect if the other man didn't feel like he could say more since he wasn't technically an officer anymore. He knew everything Walters did tell him today was a favor.

"Speaking of that subject though, could I ask you a few questions, Miss Dawson?"

"You can call me Summer." She sat up a little straighter, leaned forward a little, Clay noticed.

"Alright. Summer, do you have any idea who might want to attack you?"

The man didn't pull punches; Clay liked that.

She shook her head, as Clay had already known she would.

"I have no idea. I'm working on…compiling a list of suspicions I have."

"Of people the killer could be?" The detective raised his eyebrows. "I didn't realize you were being so proactive."

Summer laughed it off, which Clay appreciated. He didn't feel the other man needed to know the effort Summer, and he by extension, planned to go to find a link between her and the other victims. Since it wouldn't impede the official investigation and might yield useful clues, some things were just better left unsaid.

"I'm working on figuring out possible ways the killer might have met me. Things like that. I thought that might help?"

"It might. It's worth a try as long as you're staying out of danger." He looked at Clay. "Do you have her in a safe house?"

He shook his head. "The situation in Moose Haven currently makes more sense if we don't. I know you've talked to her brother Chief Noah Dawson, and he'll change her protection plan if it seems our current plan isn't sufficient."

"She has someone with her 24/7 though. Right?"

Clay nodded. "Yes, sir."

"Good." The other man looked relieved, Clay noted. He was glad that the Anchorage police were taking the threat as seriously as they were, liked that someone else had Summer's back, even if it was from a distance.

"Can you tell me in your own words what happened last night?" he asked Summer.

Summer did so and Clay listened, impressed at the way she was able to share everything with so much confidence, apparently unaffected. He knew better than to believe she was as nonchalant as she seemed. He knew how much the idea of someone being after her shook her.

But he appreciated how she was able to deliver information in a detached sort of way.

When she'd finished giving her answer, the detective nodded and then slowly stood. "I'm going to pass this information on to the rest of the team. I can't tell you how much I appreciate you coming up. I know it's a long drive."

"We have other things to do in Anchorage anyway," Summer said with a smile. Clay tried not to react but wished she hadn't shared that particular tidbit.

Thankfully the detective didn't ask questions, he just saw them out politely and then they were climbing back into Clay's car.

"That went well, right?" Summer asked when they were both buckled in.

"It did." Though it hadn't been quite as informative as he had hoped. For the first time since he'd left Georgia, Clay honestly wished he had his badge back. He'd love to know what was going on in the police department right now, what leads were going to be pursued with the new information they'd been provided. He had guesses, of course, based on how he would handle it, but that wasn't the same thing as knowing.

He was surprised by how much his civilian status stung.

He glanced over at Summer. Was it endangering her, being protected by someone who didn't have the full power of the law behind him? It was better than nothing for sure, but he'd have to talk with Noah. The other man had floated the idea of Clay being sworn in as a Moose Haven reserve officer once, but Clay had brushed him off.

Maybe it was time to accept that offer. Anything that would keep Summer safer.

* * *

Summer gave Clay the address of the first house she wanted to visit. That of the first victim's parents. Not every victim had relatives living in the state, so it worked out well for Summer that the first one had. She wanted to start at the beginning, talk to people who knew the victims while following the order of their disappearances just in case that was somehow significant.

The farther into the neighborhood they drove the heavier the pit in Summer's stomach grew. She reached for the thermos of tea she'd brought and took a sip. Luke-warm. She winced. She'd known when she came up with this idea that it would be difficult, tracing the killer's movements from one grieving family to another. Especially when her own emotions seemed to be waging a war between thankfulness that she was alive, that her family wasn't one on the list, and at the same time feeling guilty. Why her? Why was she alive when these other women were dead?

Classic survivor's guilt, Summer knew and was able to acknowledge. But it didn't change the weight that seemed to sit on her, that made it a little harder to breathe. And also drove her to answer the whispered question from somewhere inside herself. *It doesn't matter why. You're alive. What are you going to do about it?*

What was she going to do?

"Which way here?" Clay asked.

Summer smiled at the irony of his timing. "Turn left," she said after looking down at the directions she'd pulled up on her phone.

Working at the lodge was the right thing to do, she told herself as they approached the first house. There had to be a way to make it feel more like her passion.

She already knew it was worth doing because it made her family happy and family was important, that was a lesson she should have learned long ago.

She wasn't going to make that mistake again.

"This one?" Clay nodded toward a blue two-story house.

"Yes." He pulled into the driveway.

She didn't move, didn't unbuckle. She suddenly couldn't. Summer swallowed hard, tried to remind herself of all the reasons this was a good idea. Maybe their only chance.

"Ready?" Clay asked, his voice gentle and not pressuring. She smiled a little even as she still fought to keep herself from spiraling into panic.

"I'm not sure."

"Nervous?"

"I don't know what I am. Too many emotions to name, I guess."

He nodded. "I understand."

"You do?"

"It's hard to face someone who's been through this kind of tragedy, much less to ask them questions. Your part in this case, the fact that you're not just someone investigating, that's got to make it harder."

She nodded.

He started to reach his hand over, then seemed to remember earlier and pulled it back.

Summer took his, accepted the squeeze he gave once she had and gave him a small smile. "I can use all the encouragement I can get right now."

"I think what you're doing is smart."

"You're coming with me, right?" The thought of facing the family without Clay hadn't occurred to her.

"Yes," he answered before she could worry any longer. She exhaled, let go of his hand and opened the car door. "I'm ready as I'll get."

She crossed the driveway and followed the sidewalk up to the small front deck of the house. Without hesitating, because she suspected if she hesitated she'd get back into the car and ask Clay to drive straight back to Moose Haven, she knocked on the door.

Waited.

The door opened slightly and a woman she'd guess to be in her midfifties looked at both of them. "Yes?" Summer detected a slight European accent, something that was common in Anchorage and other parts of Alaska. In this woman's voice, it sounded almost musical.

"Mrs. Hunt?"

"Yes?"

She opened the door slightly farther after they mentioned her name. Summer realized she shouldn't waste time before explaining who they were. The woman's life had just been changed by violence. She was probably going to be slightly suspicious of anyone she didn't know.

"I'm Summer Dawson. I wanted to ask you some questions about your daughter." The words spilled out before she could decide if that was the best way to approach saying who she was.

"Jenna?"

"Yes." Summer nodded.

"The police have been here. You're not the police."

"No. I'm not. I'm…" She weighed her options, then decided to take a chance with full honesty. "Police think the same man tried to kill me."

Her eyes and the door both widened. "Come in. And your friend?"

"Clay. He's a former police officer who's my full-time protection at the moment."

The older woman nodded and moved aside.

Summer walked inside the house.

"Please, have a seat." She motioned to a couch and Summer sat. Clay sat beside her. She was grateful for the fire in the fireplace, since she'd started to shiver slightly. While she wasn't convinced it was from the weather, since it wasn't cold or rainy outside, the heat might help anyway.

Mrs. Hunt sat across from them. "Why don't you tell me why someone who isn't a police officer needs to ask me questions."

Summer weighed her words. She hadn't counted on how difficult it would be to talk to people who had been so personally affected by the man who was after her. Here she was, doing what she'd planned, taking charge and getting involved, and right now all she could do was sit there.

"I just… I need to see if I can find any answers to explain why this is happening. Maybe help find the man responsible."

The other woman studied her. "You seem, Summer, like the kind of person who has her own grief. You're careful in how you talk to me. I can tell that."

Avoiding Clay's eyes, Summer shrugged. The woman could read people, Summer would give her that. But she wasn't there to talk about past griefs. She wasn't even there to make the woman feel better about her own, though if she somehow could she'd certainly be happy to know she had done so. She was there for answers.

Mrs. Hunt shifted in her seat, leaned forward and

rested her elbows on her legs in a graceful gesture. "Tell me about yourself first."

"Um…" Summer fumbled for words. This wasn't how this was supposed to go. She had her questions, on another page of her notebook, written down, ready to show how she could help in this investigation rather than being the one person everyone else was protecting. Not that she minded being kept alive—she appreciated that part. But she was tired of being treated with kid gloves. Again.

If only it was the first time people had seen her as a victim. At least this time she wasn't to blame. That first time, she'd been a victim of her own life choices.

"Please." The older woman smiled and Summer sighed.

"I'm twenty-eight. I live in Moose Haven, with my family. We run a lodge." She glanced at Clay, noticing how carefully he seemed to be listening. Did he want to know more about her? Summer knew it was silly to wonder. It wasn't as though anything could come of any possible interest. But she still wanted to know—did he have any interest in her? Or did he just see her like so many other people did at the moment, as someone to protect?

She turned her attention back to Mrs. Hunt. "I love Alaska. It seemed like your daughter did too from her Facebook profile."

Mrs. Hunt nodded. "She was a fan of yours, you know."

"Of mine?" Summer shook her head. "I haven't done anything in years."

"But you were a mountain runner back in the day, weren't you? Jenna followed your career. You weren't too far apart in age and she was amazed at all you accomplished, starting with those records you broke back in high school."

Once again, the tables were uncomfortably turned. Summer had researched this victim and her family but it had never dawned on her they would know details about her life.

"I was. Yes."

"You still are."

"Why do you say that?" Why was this woman insisting on talking about Summer?

"I think it's a gift God gave you. You can't just ignore it. It's still part of who you are."

Summer didn't know what to say.

Mrs. Hunt smiled slightly. "I just felt like I was supposed to tell you that. Now, let me tell you about my Jenna."

For the next ten minutes she shared information about her daughter. Summer didn't think that all of it was relevant to the investigation, though she supposed there was a chance it could prove useful later. But a lot of what she said did pique her interest. She and Jenna had been in a lot of the same circles, even though they had never met. She ran 5Ks, hiked almost every weekend, rain or shine, and many of her favorite hikes were Summer's favorites too. She wrote a note to herself in her notebook to follow up on that possible lead. Did they both hike those mountains consistently enough that someone could have targeted them both because of it? And did the other victims share their love for those hikes?

If anything, this visit was leaving her with more questions than answers, but at least Summer felt like they were making progress. They were on the right track.

"I appreciate you talking to us today," Summer said as she finally stood. "It was extremely helpful."

"I hope something helps you find who is behind this."

Mrs. Hunt shuddered. "I don't know if I'll ever feel like the world is a safe, good place again, but him not roaming the streets would go a long way toward that."

"I understand." Summer smiled sympathetically. And she did.

Clay stood also and walked to the door before Summer, to check for threats outside, she assumed. He stepped out before she did and walked down the steps of the front deck, not far but close enough to give her a tiny bit of privacy with the woman she'd felt an unexpected connection with.

"Dear." Mrs. Hunt laid a hand on Summer's arm as Summer started to step through the front door. "Could you do something for me?"

"If it's within my capabilities, of course. I really appreciate the information you gave me today."

Mrs. Hunt didn't say anything for a minute. Summer started to prompt her for an answer, since Clay was still walking toward the car in the driveway and she felt she needed to hurry.

But then the older woman met her eyes. When she did speak, her voice was slow, gentle, firm. "My daughter… she's with Jesus now. She knew Him. But her time here is finished. Yours isn't, Summer."

Summer's eyes stung as tears started to gather at the edges.

"Here is what I'd like you to do for me. For Jenna." Now Mrs. Hunt's eyes were watering. She didn't break her gaze though, kept her eyes straight on Summer's and Summer couldn't look away. "I want you to *live*, dear. Really, truly live without regrets. Fully. Freely."

There was no need to ask what she meant, to think about how her life would change if she did that. Summer already knew. Instead, she nodded. She owed it to the woman and the daughter she'd lost.

To herself. To the tiny unborn baby daughter *she* had lost three years ago.

"I promise."

TEN

Summer had been quiet since they'd left the Hunts' house. Clay had driven her to several more places after that, but so far no one had answered the door. He didn't know if they were just not responding to people they didn't know or if they'd left town until the man behind the death of their loved ones had been caught. Either would make sense.

Someone finally answered at the fourth house they drove to.

It was the sister of one of the victims. "Who are you?" was the first thing she said when Summer knocked on the door.

"I'm trying to learn about your sister."

The door shut most of the way.

"The same man who killed her is trying to kill me."

Even Clay caught his breath at Summer's words, at the reality of them and the way they didn't pull any punches. The woman at the door blinked, opened it wider. "Come in."

The conversation that followed was much like the one with Mrs. Hunt, in Clay's opinion. They didn't learn anything new, just what they knew already. The woman said that her sister, Amanda, had lived with her, but had been on a camping trip in Chugach State Park, the mountains behind Anchorage, when she'd disappeared, and then her body had been found a few days later.

"Did she hike often?" Summer asked with a frown.

"Every weekend and at least two days a week after work in the summer. She loved all outdoorsy kinds of things." A small smile escaped the woman's face. "She'd just started to learn stand-up paddleboarding. Amanda was just always outside." The smile disappeared. "Are the police any closer to discovering who did this?"

"Aren't they keeping in touch with you with updates?"

"They are," she admitted. "But there haven't been any lately. I've been wondering if they're even still working on this or if they've given up."

The frustration in her tone was evident, and Clay guessed that the kind of helplessness she was feeling must be grating.

"They'll let you know," Clay told her with confidence.

"But you must not trust them to do their jobs, either, if you're out trying to get clues or other information."

Summer looked at Clay. Both of them seemed to be thinking. Summer was the first to shake her head slowly. "No, I do trust them. But I can't sit by and be nothing more than a victim. I can't be helpless. I've got to do something."

"So this is for you."

Summer nodded. "It's for me."

It was another glimpse into the kind of person she was, and Clay admired her more for it. To say that she trusted the police—and to mean it, Clay could tell she did—but to also know herself well enough to know when she needed to do something… Summer was thoughtful, self-aware and brave. And beautiful, not that he was supposed to be noticing that.

If they weren't in the middle of this case, he might be close to admitting that she intrigued him more than the sister of a friend really should. Might be close to admitting that in normal circumstances, he'd have asked her on a date by now, tried to figure out if she felt the same fascination with him that he did with her.

"Thanks for your time," Summer said and they walked back to the car. "Gorgeous view," she commented before they climbed in.

They'd driven up to an area of Anchorage that Summer had told him on the way there was called The Hillside. "There are tons of hillsides here. What about those houses, are those on The Hillside?" He'd pointed to a cluster of large, nice homes on a hillside up against the mountains.

She shook her head. "Stuckagain Heights."

"But they're on a hillside," he'd teased, and it was one of the lightest moments they'd had in days. They'd needed the levity, both of them. Human beings were only meant to sustain the intensity they'd been running at for short periods of time. They were both dangerously close to running out of steam.

Now, as Clay maneuvered the car carefully back down the mountainside, he kept his eyes on the road rather than take in the view.

"Clay."

Summer's voice was tense, short, and he chanced a quick look in her direction before returning his eyes to the road. "What's wrong?" He couldn't see any obvious answers. She seemed fine.

"The car behind us. He keeps getting closer."

"Is it a man behind the wheel? Can you see him?" There was still the possibility that the car behind them was an innocent bad driver.

But if it wasn't, at least Clay wanted to know if they could identify him.

"I can't really tell, but I think it's a man."

"You can't tell?"

"His windshield is tinted, I think? Or maybe it's the way the sun is hitting. But no, I can't see anything clearly distinguishing. I'm sorry. Do you think it's him?"

"I don't know." He glanced in the rearview mirror. Summer was right, Clay couldn't see anything, either, except the fact that someone was in the driver's seat. "Could be?" He took a left on the next road that would lead them to town, twisting around a hairpin turn.

Did the car edge closer?

Clay hit the gas, accelerating a little.

"What are you doing?"

"I'm not going to keep going slow and risk him hitting us here."

He twisted around the curve, looked down the road that lay head of them. After this stretch of road there was only one more spot where losing control of the car would be truly disastrous.

He came up to that danger spot, tightened his grip on the wheel and glanced in the rearview.

The car was accelerating. And Clay had nowhere to go. He didn't dare risk speeding up here lest he send them careening over the mountainside without any help from whomever was tailing them.

"Hang on, Summer!"

The car behind them hit them, lurched them forward, and Clay fought to maintain control as their car slid right, toward the guardrail, barely clipping it. The mountain-side dropped off there, and Clay knew if they hit the rail too hard, he wouldn't be able to keep their car on the road.

He jerked the wheel hard left, hitting the car that had been behind them as it sped up and disappeared down the road that led down the hillside. He tried to catch a glimpse of the license plate, but all he noticed was that it was an Alaska tag, one of the gold ones with blue numbers, which he couldn't read because it was covered in mud. That didn't narrow it down much.

The threat gone, Clay slowed their car to a stop, pulling as close to the side of the road as he dared. Exhaled.

Looked at Summer. She was crying.

"Are you okay?"

"I'm just ready for this to be over. I don't understand how someone could want another human being dead, especially not the way this guy does." She let out a shuddering breath and Clay wanted to hold her hand, maybe pull her to him, tell her it would be okay.

But he couldn't. He hadn't earned the right. And anyway, he couldn't stay here on the side of the road. They needed to report a crime—and they needed to move away from this location, in case the killer was still watching them.

But even if they'd had all the time in the world, and he'd had every right to comfort her, he wouldn't have been able to tell Summer that everything would be okay.

Because Clay didn't know if it would be or not.

He drove straight to the police department, not just because the attack needed to be reported, but also because he knew if their attacker decided to follow them again, he almost certainly wouldn't follow them to the police department. Clay might not be able to control the madman who was after Summer, nor was he really able to minimize the danger to her nearly as much as he'd like to, but he could give her a few minutes of safety at the police department, a few minutes to catch her breath.

And then they'd have to face reality again.

They were met once more by Detective Walters and Clay gave him a quick rundown of what had happened. He motioned for them to follow him to his office again and they both did so. This time another officer appeared and asked if Summer wanted coffee or tea. She asked for tea and when the officer brought it back, Summer held it tightly, like the warmth of the drink in her hand was comforting her.

Clay had turned down the refreshments. He couldn't drink anything at a time like this, couldn't relax in the slightest when the threat level had risen once again. How many more times could Summer weather an attack like that? Statistically speaking, how many close calls could they have before they didn't escape alive?

Clay didn't want to think about it. Instead he made himself think through what needed to be done, starting with other people who could be in danger.

He looked up at the officer. "Can you send a car over to check on Amanda Holbrook's sister? We were followed from her house."

The officer nodded and left to arrange it. Clay waited with Summer, who was quiet, eyes wide. She took a long sip of tea and then put the cup in front of her again, holding it in both hands and staring straight ahead.

"What?" It didn't seem right to ask what was wrong when the answer to that question was unfortunately more obvious than he'd like it to be. But it seemed like something more was bothering her than just the attack itself.

"I can't believe we might have put her in danger." She shook her head.

"No, we didn't, you didn't. No one did except the deranged man who is behind this." Clay had more he wanted to say, but he kept it short, knowing from experience that direct messages were the best for this situation. She was still too shaken for more detailed explanations.

Fortunately they soon learned that Amanda Holbrook was safe. APD promised they'd ramp up patrols in her neighborhood also and communicate with her on an even more regular basis given how doubtful she'd been.

As for Summer, they offered her a safe house in Anchorage, but she refused, as he'd known she would. Clay didn't know if she didn't fully grasp the severity of the danger or if she just didn't want to live that way no matter what. But he understood.

"Be careful." One of the officers told him as he left the building with Summer.

"I will be."

I'm running out of time to solve this, God. We all are, I can feel it. Clay prayed as they walked to the car, which was still mechanically sound, just a little dented from their hair-raising ordeal. *Help us figure this out before anyone else ends up hurt, or dead.*

He looked over at Summer. Much as he might want to deny it, it wasn't just professionalism that made him pray that prayer with her in mind specifically.

His heart couldn't handle losing her.

Summer closed her eyes in the car, letting Anchorage disappear in the rearview mirror without her paying attention. She felt the curves of the road as the car swung around the Seward Highway between the mountain cliffs and Turnagain Arm. She'd had friends in Anchorage back when she was a competitive mountain runner, and had made the drive many times to visit them and to train on some of the nearby mountains—O'Malley, Wolverine, Ptarmigan and the like.

Now this drive that was so familiar, which should have been relaxing, was another source of tension for her. She hadn't put any of it into words for Clay, but the knowledge that there were two hours of no-man's-land ahead of them scared her—nothing but the road, with no houses, no stores and no cell phone reception.

There, she'd said it. She was scared of something.

Scared that the man who wanted her dead would succeed. Scared of how much she was getting used to Clay's presence. Scared of the fact that one way or another, this arrangement with him as her bodyguard couldn't last forever, and then what was she going to do? Tell him that despite the fact that she didn't deserve a man like him, she was starting to...

What? Fall in love with him?

She shook the thoughts away. Surely it was too soon for that, even for someone like her who felt so deeply, gave her heart away so freely. Summer would have laughed aloud at the ridiculousness of the situation, except she wanted Clay to think she was asleep. She didn't trust herself to have a normal conversation right then. The sky was dimming as the clouds moved in and it grew closer to midnight. Even though the sun wouldn't disappear completely, there was something about the end of the day that made her relaxed and vulnerable. Made her want to answer Clay's unspoken questions about why she'd stopped competitive mountain running. About her past.

And that couldn't happen.

It just couldn't.

She shifted in her seat slightly so she'd have a view out of the window. The water was calm today. She'd seen it before when the rain was falling and it churned in slate gray that looked more like some kind of molten lava than water. Angry. Thick.

Today it was calm, the exact opposite of how her heart felt.

She turned her thoughts somewhere productive, wondering once again who could be after her. Even though she'd been attacked in Moose Haven, it seemed more likely the culprit was someone from Anchorage since his first victims had been from there. What had made him come to Moose Haven? Had he come specifically to target her, or had he found her after he arrived? Which had come first? Knowing that would give them somewhere to start.

The problem with trying to put together any kind of suspect list was that there was no knowing how the serial killer's mind worked—what connection he saw between the women he made into his victims. Summer didn't know if this particular killer was targeting people he knew well—she hoped it wasn't that one; she only knew a few people in Anchorage, and she couldn't picture any of them being behind this.

If he was someone who killed people he'd only seen in passing, then the possibilities were limitless. It could be someone she'd passed at Costco in Anchorage, someone who got gas at a gas station where all of the victims and Summer had been before.

Another impossibility to think through.

The third option was the one that intrigued Summer. If the killer was killing acquaintances…that was something she needed to think through. What acquaintances did she have who might have run across the other women as well? She'd been preparing a list to share with law enforcement if they were interested in it, though so far it was limited to mountain running friends and the barista at her favorite coffee shop, who she very much doubted had a mean bone in his body. Not to mention, the body type didn't match her attacker at all. Summer could probably bench-press the barista—he was tall and thin and the essence of a hipster right to the thick glasses that sat on the end of his nose.

Yeah, it wasn't him.

She kept thinking. If this option was right though, it had to be someone. She went to the post office often. Anchorage Outdoor Gear. A local knife shop that carried her favorite kind of custom knives, which she carried with her on hikes when she took tourists, because they were so useful to have in the woods.

The last one caught her attention the most. She tapped out a quick text to Noah, hoping it would send when they came back into service. For now they were entering the longest dead zone of the trip. Summer shuddered. The word *dead* wasn't her favorite lately.

She looked over at Clay, who had kept quiet, giving her space to think. She almost said something but then she closed her eyes again and pretended to sleep.

It was probably better for both of them if she kept pretending. Not just to sleep—but not to care about this intriguing man next to her who fascinated her more than she wanted to admit.

ELEVEN

Clay gripped the steering wheel as he took the hill up into Turnagain Pass. They'd been back on the Kenai Peninsula for less than half an hour, and still had well over an hour to go before they made it back to Moose Haven. Clay wished he could teleport them there—his nerves were shot after the day they'd had.

He turned the CD up—neither the radio nor streamed music on his phone worked there, he'd discovered the first time he'd driven through the massive dead zone extended from the start of the Kenai all the way to Moose Pass, the tiny town just before the turnoff to Moose Haven.

Five or ten minutes after Turnagain Pass—he hadn't been keeping track of time but it hadn't been long—he spotted upcoming construction, dropping his speed as the signs dictated. He didn't remember it being there this morning, but he'd heard orange construction cones bloomed in Alaska like the state flower in the summer so it shouldn't be surprising.

He took advantage of the break from driving fast to look around. The scenery was some of the most gorgeous he'd ever seen, vast wilderness covered by spruce trees.

On the right side of the road was a creek, with a hill be-hind it that gradually climbed toward the mountains.

Gorgeous. But also desolate.

Clay shivered as he looked around. He saw no other vehicles on the road. He looked at the construction cones, narrowed his eyes.

It could be legitimate construction. But if so, he was going to have to make some apologies to whoever caught him doing this.

He hit the gas, unable to shake the unease he felt slow-ing down in this isolated area.

The first *bang* told him he was too late. The front left tire blew. The shooter was on Clay's side of the car, hid-den somewhere in the woods.

Summer's head snapped up. "What was that?"

Another shot.

"We've got to ditch the car. Summer, when I stop, open your door, jump out and run into the woods. I'm right behind you." Clay had spent a lot of time in the woods hunting deer and knew more about long-range rifle shots than most people, law enforcement or not. The shooter wasn't particularly close—which was good because it gave them a better chance to escape from him personally, but bad because if he was this accurate a shot from far away, they were in a huge amount of danger.

Clay hit the breaks.

"Run?"

"Now! Run!"

Clay searched the woods to his left for anything that would give away the shooter's location—maybe a reflec-tion of the scope in the sun, anything. He saw nothing but heard Summer's door.

She was out and he needed to be with her.

He opened his door, ran for the back of the car. One more shot—this one took out the back tire. Clay heard it explode just as he made it past, running for the other side of the car and sprinting off the road, into the thick woods.

"Summer?" he shouted, hating to give away her position but knowing that whoever was shooting at them already knew they were together, and that it was worth the risk to get back to where she was so he could protect her.

"Right here!"

Ahead of him, slightly to the right. He dodged a spruce branch, rounded that tree and saw a game trail. "Game trail?"

"I saw it. To your left. Don't take it, it's the first thing he'll check."

She was right but he wouldn't have realized she'd know that.

"How'd you know?"

"My sister, Kate. She's the best tracker. She's taught me a few things. I figured some of it could come in handy if we use it backward. I've already made a couple false trail starts."

She might be the most amazing woman he'd ever met.

"Is he following us?" she asked, not slowing down as she ran. Clay ran too but struggled to keep up—Summer's strides were that effortless. Then again, she did this often for fun, didn't she?

He resolved again to make running part of his daily routine. Assuming they both lived through this to have a daily routine again.

"No way of knowing."

Clay glanced backward though, just in case. This time he caught the sun reflecting off something that looked to be about seven hundred yards away.

Clay guessed he'd made the shot from about five hundred yards, somewhere up there on that mountainside. A shot not every accomplished marksman could make when they were shooting at a moving target the size of his tires.

The big question was, was he moving? Clay still couldn't tell but knew he had to assume the answer was yes—which meant they couldn't stop or they'd risk being targeted again. He kept running.

Turned around again. Nothing.

"Clay?" Summer's voice was desperate. She'd stopped running.

"Keep going. I'll catch up to you." He needed to know.

Long seconds stretched into almost a minute before he caught another flash.

Fifty yards closer.

He was coming for them.

Clay sprinted up the hill, following Summer's footsteps.

She exhaled. Blew out a breath. "We can't just keep sprinting. We have to be smarter."

"Where are we?" Clay hated that he was reliant on someone else's knowledge, but he just didn't have the backcountry familiarity that Summer did.

All the sudden he was struck by how much he needed her. Here this whole time he'd been thinking of himself as her rescuer, her protector, but she'd brought him back into law enforcement, given him daily purpose again when he'd been struggling and now was half the reason they weren't in more danger than they already were.

Summer Dawson was not just another woman to protect.

"We should be crossing a creek soon."

"You can tell that?"

She smiled. "I've studied maps. I've hiked fairly near here. Not precisely here," she warned. "So I don't know exactly what we're getting into, but I may know enough that we have a chance."

"Okay, which creek?"

Summer shook her head. "I'm not sure, especially since I was asleep, so I'm not positive of our exact location. Either Silvertip Creek or Six Mile Creek. If we follow Six Mile we'll end up at a rest stop, near the Hope Cutoff."

Clay remembered that road, one that led to the small town of Hope. "So we have options for contacting civilization if we can get to either of those locations."

"It'll be a long hike. But yes. The rest stop has an emergency phone."

"I hear the creek."

It was wide enough to give Clay some pause, especially as it ran cold and fast like most creeks in Alaska. A slip in one of those could be deadly.

"Let's go." Clay broke his hesitation and stepped in. Summer followed.

"He's coming, isn't he?"

"Why?"

"You've gotten faster."

"Maybe I just wanted to keep up with you."

"Nah. You're running like it matters." Summer made her way across the creek with the calm aplomb of an Alaskan woman who'd done this many times before. Clay was still dealing with the shock the cold water was to his legs but continued on.

Then they were out.

"Up?" Summer asked.

The landscape in front of them rose dramatically to a lower mountain ridge that connected to a bigger mountain that loomed in front of them.

"Yes. Let's go."

They ran without talking anymore, both of them sweating at this point even in the mild temperatures.

"I really hope we don't startle a bear. We should be making noise."

"It's a risk we have to take. I'd rather meet a bear than whoever's at the other end of that gun."

Summer turned and met his eyes before she kept running. "I don't want to meet either."

Summer ran like she was in the World Mountain Running Championships and victory was on the line. But there was so much more at stake than that here. The adrenaline coursing through her, it was all wrong. Running had never been a method of escape for her, she'd never run *from* anything. Always *to* something. Like her dreams.

Then again, hadn't she been running from her past for years? Running from the memories of when her dream career almost came true?

She stopped when she noticed something in the trees. The light was changing, getting brighter. She turned to Clay, who was keeping pace well, even if he did seem winded.

"We're almost out of the tree line. We need to head one direction or another along the edge of it or we'll be back in plain sight again."

"We need to stay out of his sight, that's what's most important right now."

"That's what I figured. So left or right?"

She waited for him to decide. Left took them toward Moose Haven; right took them back toward Anchorage. Neither place was close enough to walk to. On one hand, she guessed the killer might expect them to head toward the Hope Cutoff on the left, but then again it was impossible to know for sure what he'd be expecting. It wasn't worth making a bad choice just to try to throw him off.

She looked left, thought about Silvertip Creek and Six Mile Creek. They widened toward the Hope Cutoff, near the Canyon Creek rest stop, and the land around the creek became steeper.

Summer glanced at Clay. Should she offer her opinion, treat him like they were some kind of team, them against a serial killer? Or wait and let him do the protecting?

"What do you think?" He turned to her.

Summer smiled. She should have known he'd ask for her input. Clay Hitchcock may have drifted into Moose Haven like so many loners who came to Alaska to work short-term jobs, but he wasn't the same as they were. He was a team player, something she assumed had served him well in law enforcement.

"We need to go left, toward the cutoff."

"Left it is, then. Keep going."

Summer kept moving, careful not to trip on the roots that tangled on the forest floor. Her muscles were handling the climb fine, but her heart rate was pounding—mostly, she assumed, from the certainty that their lives were in danger.

"Where are we headed, specifically?" Clay asked after a minute.

"Do you want to keep going until we can't run anymore? Or take shelter somewhere?"

"I think we're better off taking shelter to rest after we've gone a decent distance. The town of Hope is within range of us technically but I don't know if there's a way for us to pick our way there on trails."

"I'm not sure, either. I know we are headed that way but I don't know how realistic it is to make it all the way to Hope." Summer winced. "There's bound to be a trail near the creek, at least a game trail, but that's not very sheltered and I'm hesitant to stick next to a creek when it's summer."

"Bears?"

She nodded. "And of course neither of us has bear spray."

"I've got my weapon." He patted his side.

"What is that, a .45?" She raised her eyebrows. "So if we need something noisy to try to scare the bear away we're set, but I'm afraid it's not going to help with much more than that."

"Okay, so we'll take the route you mentioned. We'll go as far as we can, take a rest and then decide where we should hike out."

"You think he'll track us for long?"

"I have no idea. I do know that as well as you know these woods we have a fighting chance. I'm not sure we would without you."

Summer loved the way he smiled at her just then, like she mattered, like she was important. "Thanks, Clay."

And just that fast, the moment was over. He nodded to the left, where they'd planned to go. "Let's go, okay. He's probably still back there."

Summer was careful not to leave much of a trace as she picked her way through the spruce trees, between them, sometimes doubling back to mess up the trail, and showing Clay how to do the same, but never straying too far because time was still important and she couldn't afford to waste too much of it on deception when they didn't even know if the man who was after them was a capable tracker.

They'd been running for well over a mile in difficult terrain, Summer would guess more like two or three, when Clay finally said they should stop.

"I think we've lost him." He glanced at his watch. "And it's getting later. I would be surprised if he searched all night."

"So we stop, then?" She shivered. As it got closer to nighttime, the daylight didn't change much, but the temperature started to drop even in the early evening, hours before.

"We stop. I'm going to build a fire to warm us up some."

"But the smoke?"

"We'll be careful. I'm not going to let it get very big so the smoke shouldn't be visible." He didn't say anything more, but somehow Summer got the idea that the reason he wasn't concerned about the smoke might be a little disconcerting to know.

"You think if he's going to find us he'll do that whether there's smoke or not."

He met her eyes and nodded slowly. "You'd make an excellent police officer, do you know that?"

She laughed. "Not my kind of danger. But thanks."

They hiked in silence for another few miles before they came to where Six Mile Creek made a large canyon lined with huge masses of rock. They were on the far side. Whether their shooter would expect that was still unknown. They had chosen to cross immediately, but there was a slight chance, Summer assumed, that he might wonder if they'd just stayed close to the road and followed it along the perimeter of the woods rather than cross the creek at all. He almost certainly wouldn't guess they'd crossed here because the rapids where the canyon walls enclosed the creek were some of the best in Alaska.

"We should stop here." Summer turned to Clay. "It's the location with the best options for places we can sort of tuck back into, and the noise of the creek will cover the noise we make moving around."

"You know best here."

They stopped running and Clay gathered what they needed to make a small fire. They would need to warm up, especially if they needed to run again.

Once he'd gotten the fire started, Clay turned to Summer. She almost looked away, but something in his expression made her meet his eyes. Wait for whatever he had to say.

"What did you mean earlier about 'your kind of danger'?"

"What?" Summer only vaguely remembered what he was talking about.

"When I said you'd make a good cop."

"Oh." She nodded once, remembering now. The words had slipped out and she wasn't sure now, in retrospect, that she'd meant to reveal so much of herself.

She considered brushing him off, dodging the question. Then again, what was the worst that could happen? Usually she'd say looks of judgment. But while Clay was a man whose character made him seem almost too good to be true, she suspected he wasn't the kind to judge other people harshly. He didn't seem critical.

"I guess I meant…" She shrugged and laughed a little. "Exactly what I said. It's not my kind of danger."

"So you have a kind?"

"I'm pretty sure you've figured out by now the whole mountain running thing isn't just a hobby for me. Or if you haven't figured it out, you've looked up my background online."

"I don't look up other people unless it's someone I'm investigating."

Summer hadn't seen that one coming. "Why not?"

"It's not fair to them. The internet is changing how relationships work. Have you realized that? Once upon a time you got to know someone little by little, with what they chose to reveal to you at each step, and now you can go on their Facebook, see their hobbies, interests, favorite music, learn about that time they went to Peru on a mission trip and got lost in the jungle, all of that is right there, from the start."

She settled back against the fallen log she'd been using as a backrest and thought for a minute before responding. Finally, she nodded. "You're right. I hadn't thought of that." She winced a little. "I looked you up a little. Just enough to see you were an officer and see what happened in what looks like your last case."

Clay nodded, like he'd been prepared for that, although she did notice his shoulders went back a little, and Summer could almost sense an invisible wall between them that hadn't been there five minutes ago. What Clay had said about the internet and friendships made even more sense now. Like her, it seemed that he had things in his past that he didn't want to share online with the whole world. She could respect that. She'd taken his chance to talk about that in real time, as their friendship grew.

Odd she'd never thought about that before.

"I'm sorry." She blew out a breath. "I do see what you mean now."

He shrugged. "It is what it is. Technology changes things. So tell me about you and mountain running. I'd figured out it had to be more than a casual interest."

"How?"

Clay laughed as he worked on the fire, placing more medium weight logs on it. "Today was the giveaway. You spent forty-five dollars on a T-shirt."

"Hey, that was the clearance price too, and totally worth it. It's not just a T-shirt. It's an Arc'teryx that's moisture wicking and technical so that it—" His expression looked remarkably like Kate's anytime Summer tried to talk about clothes, outdoor gear or not. She laughed too. "Okay, fine, so the gear gives me away."

"And your dedication," he continued. "Not to mention the way your face looks when you're running up a mountain."

She tilted her head to the side, unsure what he meant. So she sat, listening to the creek and the small crackle of the fire and waited for him to explain.

"You look like you're somewhere else, almost. It looks a lot like worship."

Summer was already shaking her head. "Worship?"

"Thanking God. Praising."

"I know what it is. I'm just curious why you think I would."

"Your brother's faith is one of the reasons we became friends in the first place. Two guys at a state school— we stuck out a little bit wanting to follow Jesus. I've talked enough with Noah to know he shares that faith. I don't know much about Kate, she's pretty busy and keeps things to herself but I've seen her Bible in the lodge in your family's area and it moves around, like she takes it different places to read."

The man really did take "observant" to a whole new level.

"And you're telling me that with three siblings who know Jesus, you honestly don't?"

Heartbeats passed. "That's not what I said, either." Summer forced the words out slowly.

They sat by the fire in silence. She didn't offer any more information. Clay didn't ask any questions.

Her shoulders fell. She wasn't giving up on escaping from this man who wanted her dead. Not by a long shot. But his silent, unknown, possible presence made everything feel heavier, made her consider everything more deeply. What if he did succeed, did manage to kill her? Was she happy with her life now?

If she died now, could she honestly say she'd been living for the last three years?

TWELVE

Clay knew he'd misstepped, at least where Summer was concerned. What he didn't know was how, exactly. He'd assumed up until now that Summer might be in one of those seasons of life where she was busy and her times with God were inconsistent, but it appeared she intentionally avoided God.

As a police officer, Clay had seen more than his share of how life could break people. He'd seen people who had let tragedy push them to vices. Drugs. Alcohol. It wouldn't surprise him if Summer used mountain running to escape in the same way. What he didn't know was how to convince her that he understood, that he didn't think worse of her because she wasn't living in her faith right now. He was sad for her. But it didn't change his opinion of her.

"What did my brother tell you about me?"

"What do you mean?" Clay asked in an attempt to stall for time, to give himself a minute to figure out how to react to her question. This was the kind of conversation he hadn't anticipated ever having with Summer. They were friends. Bodyguard and woman in danger. It wasn't that the topic was anything too intimate, but it was certainly personal, more personal a conversation than he'd have guessed they would be having.

How long was he going to have to tell himself those things until he finally and truly believed it?

He met her glacier-blue eyes, swallowing hard at the knot in his throat that had nothing to do with this particular conversation and everything to do with the draw he felt toward her.

Summer took a breath and continued, "I was under the impression somehow, when we first met, that he'd told you about me."

"Just that you were his sister and to stay away from you."

"That's what I thought."

Her voice had hardened. Interesting. Why?

Clay shook his head, not sure what he was reassuring her about, but wanting to anyway. "I don't think he meant anything bad by it."

Her laugh was hard, cold. "Sure he didn't. I get it, okay, Clay? You're this great guy. You've got real faith. Guys like you deserve women who believe as strongly as you do."

"There you go again, talking about yourself like you don't know Jesus when you haven't answered my question yet about whether or not you do. Are you a Christian, Summer?"

He wasn't usually so blunt, didn't usually feel it was the best approach, but Summer was pushing him toward it. Maybe she was pushing to see if he'd give up on her? He wasn't sure but he could tell she was going for some kind of reaction. He didn't know if it was best to give it to her or not, but the woman touched such a raw place inside him, ignited his emotions to such a degree that he didn't want to measure what he said, didn't want to keep his distance anymore and keep his feelings uninvolved.

Honestly he wanted to kiss away every frown line on her face that said she didn't think she was good enough. Good enough for *whom*? She was the kind of woman who was so hopelessly out of his league he had hardly allowed himself to consider her.

"I asked Jesus to save me when I was seven," she said softly. "Told him I knew I was a sinner. That I believed His death on the cross was for me too. And I did, Clay." She sniffed. He didn't know if she was crying or if the smoke was bothering her. So Clay didn't do anything, just waited.

But after a long moment of silence, he finally prompted her, "And?"

She smiled wryly. "My faith may be a bit…lapsed at the moment, but I know that's all that's required. What do you mean, 'and'?"

"Something happened to take the childlike faith of a seven-year-old and dampen it, push it aside."

Summer let out a breath. "Even if you had looked me up I guess you wouldn't know this part."

"I told you I didn't. I don't know anything about you that you haven't told me. Besides that your brother wanted you to be off-limits—but, Summer, I think that was because he doesn't think I'm good enough for you."

She was already shaking her head. "No, he just knows…" Her cheeks flamed. "He knows how easy it is for me when my heart gets involved to forget everything else."

Clay's chest was tight, it was getting harder to breathe. Something about the heartbreak coming off Summer was affecting him. Was this what it felt like to be really truly close to a person? He'd had a few solid friends in high school, guys from his town who he was still pretty close to today. But there was an added element here, and it was not just attraction.

He stoked the fire a little more. Looked at Summer. Her face was a mixture of so many expressions. Even though he hadn't pressured her to share anything, he felt like he should step back, give her a chance to see if she wanted to continue this story. He had a feeling it wasn't one she told often.

"I'm going to take a quick walk around."

"Without me?"

"I'll be within sight at all times," he promised. "I just want to check the perimeter, basically make sure I don't see any signs that someone's hiding."

She blinked. "Okay."

He nodded. Walked away. Whatever happened between them or didn't, Clay never wanted her to feel anything resembling pressure. This story was a piece of Summer. If she wanted to share it, it was a piece he'd accept, whatever it held. But Clay needed to know she'd thought through what they were doing, the way they were quickly crossing the line into a relationship that wasn't in any way superficial anymore, was barely resembling professional at this point, though it was still completely appropriate.

Clay's check of the woods around them didn't yield anything, which was reassuring but also concerning. Was it too quiet? Or was he just jumpy? Clay still had no way of knowing whether the shooter would come after them again tonight. On one hand, it was logical to assume their shooter had a plan of attack—a reason why he had chosen to strand them in this desolate place. On the other, he might have assumed animals or exposure would ensure they didn't make it out of the woods alive, even if he didn't personally follow them far.

Only time would tell. And Clay was a patient man. He could wait.

He just wished for Summer's sake that he could re-assure her.

Instead he sat back down near her and the fire, and glanced over at her.

Her emotions weren't written as plainly on her face anymore, the familiar mask had come back over it. He expected that was the end of that.

"I ran off with another mountain runner."

The words had no preamble, nothing to soften the blow.

"He wasn't a Christian, and my parents and especially my siblings made it clear how they felt about me giving up on what I'd been taught, leaving with him, living with him…" Her voice trailed off and Clay heard what she left unsaid. He had no idea what to say. There didn't seem to be anything he could say to encourage her, and he could feel that she wasn't done—she was just giving it to him in parts the best she knew how.

"They warned me." She blew out a breath. "They told me nicely, harshly, any way they thought I'd listen, all of them taking turns playing good cop and bad cop, really." Summer shook her head. "I put them through so much and I didn't even know it at the time." She shrugged as a tear, only one, ran down the edge of her cheek. "I didn't think about it."

"People usually don't."

"Anyway. I pushed them away enough that they finally left me alone. And I was happy. I thought *we* were happy. And then…"

Clay's stomach rolled. He thought he could feel what was coming next.

"I got pregnant. But…"

She didn't pause long enough for the words to sink into Clay's mind before she kept going. He fought to stay focused, keep his mind from spinning, asking questions he didn't know if he should ask aloud or leave unsaid. *God help her tell me what You want her to share.* He finally managed to form the words to a prayer in his mind. It was all he could think to do.

"I lost the baby. Miscarried at thirteen weeks."

He didn't know much about babies but did some quick math. Three months? And the whole pregnancy was only supposed to last nine? He thought he recalled that the risk of losing a baby usually happened in the first trimester. She'd been a third of the way there, out of the woods…

"He had a new girlfriend by the time I got out of the hospital." Her emotions had shuttered again, her eyes revealed nothing in the darkening light. "I couldn't run for a couple of months due to complications. By the time I was physically ready to get back to it, my family needed me. I owed them an apology that was more than just words. The lodge was in trouble so I came back, hoping the tiny bit of fame I had leftover would be enough to give the hikes we offer at Moose Haven Lodge an edge over some of our competition, especially the bigger chain resorts. If I'd helped out the summer they'd asked me to, rather than leaving with Christopher, the lodge might never have been in trouble to begin with…" Her voice trailed off.

Another exhale. "And that's why he wanted you to

stay away from me. I'm not the kind of woman you deserve."

"What makes you so sure? You've been through more than most people your age dream about and you've come out stronger. Don't you see that? You aren't broken."

"I am, Clay." She shook her head. "I am."

He hesitated. "Fine. But if you are, it's just so God can put you back together. Stronger. Even more beautiful." He lifted her chin, softly, slightly.

He looked at her face but she wouldn't meet his eyes, kept hers on the ground. He didn't move his hand, didn't look away. Finally her eyes lifted to meet his, filling his heart with something stronger than he'd ever felt, some kind of pull, attraction that Clay had to fight with all his might to resist covering her lips with his. He wanted to kiss away the pain she'd shared, kiss away her insecurities, but it wouldn't be fair to her, to either of them. Not right now. It wasn't the right time or place. For either of them. Especially in light of all Summer had just shared. He was starting to care about her, much more than she realized, Clay was pretty sure. But she was vulnerable right now and he wouldn't take advantage of that.

"I'm just not that woman, Clay. I don't know if I can be."

Her words fell in the quiet like weights. He could almost feel the pull of them inside his own chest, sinking any kind of hope of convincing her otherwise.

And he had to sit there, not do anything physical to convince her that she was wrong. His arms felt empty with how much he wanted to pull her close, just hold her. Tight. Maybe forever.

A gunshot broke through the air.

Clay was instantly on alert but couldn't place where it came from—except that it was close.

He finally located the spot where dirt had flown up. Just behind and to the left of Summer.

She looked up at him, eyes wide. Glanced at her leg.

And the red soaking her khaki hiking pants just below her knee.

Summer's breath came faster as she tried to process what had happened. Shot. She'd been shot.

"We have to run. Go as fast as you can. I'll find you but I need you safe." Clay's voice, so soft only moments before, supportive, understanding, was firm. He left no room for argument even though she knew he'd seen the blood spreading on her leg.

It didn't burn much, not the way she'd always heard about gunshots hurting. She didn't know if real life was that different from fiction or if she'd only been grazed.

Summer stood, hoping the second was true. She had to hold on to hope, it was all she had.

Hope. How long had it been since she'd used that word, really held on to it and believed it did any good at all?

She pushed her past out of her mind, something she was well practiced in, and did what she always did, but this time with the urgency that her life depended on it. Summer ran.

She heard footsteps behind her, hoped they were Clay's and assumed since she hadn't been shot yet that they were.

More gunshots. The big, louder kind. The man after them was still using a rifle, her experiences hunting caribou had taught her the distinct difference in the sound.

Then small caliber shots from right behind her. She glanced back. It was Clay, shooting at a dark shadow of a person maybe thirty yards away—pretty good range for a handgun.

His second shot connected with something. She heard a voice cry out.

"Go!" Clay yelled at her. "He's down, at least for now."

He was right behind her, and Summer somehow ran faster than she ever had, down the edges of the creek, toward the Hope Cutoff, careful not to slip on the rocks near the creek. *Please don't let there be bears out tonight, God.*

The second prayer that had slipped out since this ordeal had begun just three days ago.

She kept running, the dim twilight of the middle of the Alaskan night giving her just enough light to see by.

"Where do you want to cross?" They'd have to cross in order to reach the road, and at this point there was no more stopping. They'd have to find someone, someplace to make a call and have backup sent. It was all-or-nothing time.

Her heart pounded as she waited for Clay's answer, and Summer kept running.

"Whenever you think it's best."

There wasn't anywhere that was a great option. Alaska rivers and creeks ran cold and fast, and a misstep could cost a healthy adult his or her life. It had happened before, people slipping on the round, smooth rocks, then falling into the cold water and being swept away.

Even if they ever found their way out, hypothermia was quick to set in and was unforgiving.

Still, she and Clay didn't have a choice. Every chance of help they had was on the other side of Six Mile Creek.

Summer kept running until the topography changed and the solid rock cliffs gradually diminished in size and then faded entirely, giving way to land that was almost flat, leading straight down to the water.

Now or never.

Taking a deep breath and steeling herself against the cold, Summer stepped into the water. It was colder than earlier. Of course, they'd crossed at such a narrow spot earlier that they hadn't had to stay in the water too long, and the fact that the sun had been fully up in the sky had given them enough warmth to make up for the cold on their feet.

Dry, clean socks. If they made it out of this, that was what Summer wanted, even more than she wanted someone to check on her leg. That was the one advantage to the cold water. It reached high enough to numb the wound.

The water was calmer there than it had been upstream in the rapids, much calmer. Summer was pleasantly surprised at how little they had to fight with the water to hurry across it. Still, she didn't dare risk slipping by running across, but instead chose her steps carefully.

Two more and she'd be out. She glanced back to make sure Clay was making it. Her eyes widened and she realized her mistake as her foot slipped under her.

Clay caught her by the elbow and held his footing firm as Summer's stabilized. Her heartbeat pounded in her ears, a reminder of how close she'd come to falling, an accident that could have cost her everything.

"Thank you."

"Of course."

Summer took one more step in the water, then stepped out onto the shore, feeling somehow like that last brief "thank you" had been about more than just rescuing her from her fall. She was thankful to him for everything. For listening. For his protection.

For seeing her. And still…not leaving.

"Run to the highway."

Summer had been planning on it but was glad they were both on the same page. "Got it." She took a deep breath, fatigue starting to creep up on the edges of the rush of adrenaline that had overtaken her when the shot had rung out.

Running through the grass should have been easier than running down the mountain, but it wasn't what she trained for, so without the extreme adrenaline she found herself tiring out.

"Keep going, Summer. You've got this."

She pushed herself. Her leg throbbed. The more she thought about it, it had to be just a graze or she knew she couldn't run on it, but that didn't mean it didn't hurt. She'd never even been *grazed* by a bullet before.

She saw headlights in the predawn fog. The highway was close, just through a small patch of spruce trees. They kept running, and then she stopped just short of the clearing on the side of the road, still in the cover of the woods. "Do we just go out there and hope no one shoots at us?" The moon had come out from behind a cloud and was providing more light—not the best timing but not something they could change, either.

"Yes. He should still be behind us in the woods."

"But what if he's not?"

"I can't promise you anything, Summer. But he's not everywhere. And I don't think it's likely he's going to be driving by anytime soon. He has to make it down the mountain with whatever wounds he has. And we can't afford to spend too much time waiting. When we get to a phone we need to report all of this to the troopers so they can try to catch him and also give him any kind of medical assistance he needs."

She looked at him, eyes wide.

"They teach us to shoot to eliminate the threat," Clay said softly. "You don't do that, you end up with dead officers. But we also are taught to do everything we can to save a life. Even the life of someone who doesn't deserve it."

The man was a cop to his core, had he realized that yet? Summer felt a pang in her chest. When he realized it, would he leave Moose Haven, head back to his little Georgia town and the police force he'd left behind? No matter how she felt about him—something she hadn't had time to decide anyway—she didn't think she could leave to go with him. She couldn't abandon her family, or the lodge when they needed her there.

She wouldn't let history repeat itself.

THIRTEEN

Clay could hear the fear in Summer's voice, something he'd heard in it so rarely that it surprised him, though he knew it shouldn't have. She had every right to fear after what she'd been through.

So he grabbed her hand, squeezed it and smiled. "We're going to make it, Summer." And then he pulled her out of the darkness of the woods, knowing the safety they felt there was an illusion. Staying in the shadows would only endanger them.

And Clay knew it. Which was why he made his feet move even though he understood Summer's hesitations, felt them too.

The highway was mostly empty at this time of night. He glanced down at his watch, unable to tell from the deep blue of the sky how much time they had until it was good and daylight again. The deep blue was deceiving, not really darkness but not light, either. Alaskan midnight sun confused him.

It was 3:17 a.m.

The headlights continued approaching from the south. Clay hadn't been counting on anyone headed up from the Kenai at this time of night, although he guessed getting an early start to Anchorage would make sense for some people. He hoped it was that and not people who were up to no good. Even if they could get a driver to stop for them, there was no guarantee that the man or woman could be trusted—that was the risk they had to take if they had any hope of getting back to the lodge safely.

"I'm going to flag them down." Clay released Summer's hand, then clicked on the flashlight he'd had in his pocket, a small penlight that gave off enough lumens that it should be able to catch a driver's attention. He only prayed it didn't catch the attention of the man who was after them.

The car slowed slightly. Clay kept waving his arms and the light.

They moved to the side of the road, then slowed to a stop.

Clay approached with caution. "Stay behind me," he said to Summer in a quiet voice as he moved forward. The driver of the car had only lowered the window slightly and he didn't blame them. He must look odd out there in the middle of the night, no car in sight, waving.

"Can you help us, please? There's a man after us and we need a ride to Moose Haven. Or to Hope if that's all you're willing to do." Moose Haven was another hour and a half, Clay guessed. Hope should only be about fifteen or twenty minutes away.

"Who are you?"

Clay could only see part of the driver's face but it looked to be a woman in her forties. Not their shooter. Summer had identified him as a man. He was thankful for that.

"Ma'am, I know it sounds odd. But we're from Moose Haven. You can call the police chief there, Noah Dawson, and he'll tell you. I'm Clay, I work at Moose Haven Lodge and this is Summer Dawson."

The woman's face brightened. "Summer Dawson? You were a mountain runner?"

Summer nodded.

"My daughter started running cross-country because of you."

Clay heard locks on the car click and held his breath. Was she giving them a ride?

"Jump in." She nodded toward the back seat, then looked around. "But hurry, would you? If someone is after you I'd rather them not see us. I promised my husband I'd be careful on this drive. I don't think he was expecting anything other than the usual dangers and I wouldn't hear the end of it if I got shot."

"Thank you. Thank you so much," Summer said. Clay opened the back door and let her slide in first, then followed her. The woman pulled an impressive 180 in the middle of the road, since there was no traffic coming in either direction, and hit the gas.

"I'm going to call the police as soon as we have a signal," Clay told Summer.

"Shouldn't be long. Moose Pass is about thirty minutes away."

Clay had guessed longer than that. Then again, when he checked the speedometer over the driver's shoulder it said seventy-five. Not exactly what he'd consider a careful night speed, but then again, it might be best for all of them in these odd circumstances.

They rode in silence. Adrenaline was crashing in Clay, tiredness making his mind fuzzy. He knew he needed to stay focused long enough to get them safely home and talk to the police officers on the case, and he knew he would do it, but he was also looking forward to sleeping later, something he'd arrange with Noah so another officer could watch the lodge at that time. There was no way either he or Summer could hold up without one.

Just as they came into Moose Pass, the first town they reached and the last before Moose Haven, Clay's phone showed that he had service. He called the troopers first, gave the location he'd shot at the suspect and a brief explanation of what had happened. Then he called Noah.

"Clay? Is everything okay?" Noah answered his cell immediately.

"Mostly. We were shot at on the highway. Summer's got a graze on her leg and we'll need someone to look at it. We flagged down a woman, who is giving us a ride."

"Where is she bringing you?"

"Ma'am? Would you mind driving us all the way to Moose Haven Lodge or should I ask someone to meet us?" Clay asked the driver, whose name he realized he still hadn't gotten.

"I'm driving you to the lodge." She looked back over her shoulder at Summer. "My daughter really looks up to you. I couldn't face her knowing I hadn't done what I could to keep you safe. I read in the paper about the attack the other day."

Clay hadn't considered it being in the papers, but of course, especially in the small-town-feeling Kenai Peninsula, it would be widely reported.

"Thank you." Summer's voice was soft. Clay glanced at her, wondering if the words about the woman's daughter looking up to her had affected her. Unfortunately he couldn't talk about it with her right then.

He went back to his conversation with Noah. "She says she'll take us to the lodge."

"Great. I've been calling you for hours. We expected you just a few hours after dinner."

"I know. Like I said, we were ambushed on the highway and shot at."

"Just the one guy?"

"Yes, but he's got the skills of someone who's an experienced hunter or maybe former military."

Noah muttered under his breath.

"We're okay."

"Not okay enough."

Clay agreed, but he wasn't the kind of guy to get upset at circumstances he couldn't change. They were alive. Now it was time to move on.

His personal past, that last case, flashed in his mind. Was he following his own advice with that one?

No time to think about it now.

"I'm going to let you go." Noah's voice was gruff with emotion. Clay couldn't imagine being on the other end of tonight, knowing they were hours late, knowing literally anything could have happened to them.

"Alright. We'll see you soon."

"I hope so."

Clay pocketed his phone. Then remembered the man he'd shot. He dialed 9-1-1, figuring the troopers might be closer than the officers in Moose Haven.

He filled them in on the situation and the trooper he spoke to promised they'd send an officer and an ambulance to the scene.

"I'd send more than one officer," Clay advised, fearing they might be underestimating the man they were dealing with. "I don't know if he has some kind of formal training, but while I wouldn't go right to 'sniper,' he's an awfully good shot at long range."

The trooper thanked him for the information and Clay hung up. They were well through Moose Pass now, not far from Moose Haven.

As they turned off the Seward Highway, Clay noticed the deep blue of the sky had turned to a medium, vivid blue he couldn't describe but that he knew meant dawn and daylight wouldn't be far behind. He'd never been so thankful for Alaska's odd sunlight hours—somehow he just needed to see daylight right then.

The miles passed quickly as they approached the lodge. "Thank you again for the ride," Clay said as the woman pulled into the front of the lodge. Two trooper cars were waiting, as was Noah's Moose Haven cruiser and one other.

The driver whistled. "Backup is waiting, huh?"

"Yes, ma'am."

"You keep saying 'ma'am.' Where are you from? Not here." She turned to Clay.

"Georgia."

She smiled. "I guessed the South somewhere from that accent. My husband and I are originally from Athens."

"Go Dawgs." Clay smiled as he mentioned what was arguably the state's favorite football team, headquartered at the University of Georgia in Athens.

"Go Dawgs," she agreed. "You keep this woman safe, okay?"

"I'll do the best I can," Clay promised and they climbed out.

She drove away and they walked toward the entrance to the lodge. They were met by a swarm of law enforcement, a paramedic and Summer's family, all of them surrounding them, engulfing them.

Tyler grabbed Summer as soon as he saw her, hugged her tight the way Clay wished he had a right to.

"I'll be okay. Really," she said with a sniff.

Clay believed it was true. About all of it. The woman was strong, maybe the strongest he'd ever met. And certainly much stronger or braver than she knew.

If they could keep her safe for just a while longer. This guy was bound to mess up eventually, leave some evidence they could use. For all Clay knew, he might have left some already back where he'd shot at them along the highway and the creek. He'd have to have Summer give the troopers her best estimate of exactly where they'd been when the shooting had taken place. Maybe this would be the key to closing the case—and Summer not needing his protection anymore.

"I know you must be exhausted," Erynn Cooper said to Summer.

"I am." Summer's eyes were dry and it was getting harder to keep her eyelids open. At least the troopers had let an EMT see to her leg wound first. As she'd suspected it was only a graze, though a bit of a nasty one. She'd gotten worse gashes falling down scree slopes on mountains before though, so she knew she could handle it. Summer yawned. She supposed she should just be thankful that she'd had the burst of energy that enabled her to run so much that night without any rest.

"But I've got to talk to you now and get some answers while things are still fresh in your mind." Her voice was apologetic.

"Just ask her the questions, Erynn. Don't waste her time," Noah snapped as he walked up.

"Noah."

"I'm sorry." He looked at Summer, then at Erynn. "Sorry, Erynn."

"I get it, she's your sister. But you've got to keep it together if you're going to help her at all. Not to mention if you want to be part of this investigation with how close you are to it."

Summer looked at her brother, who'd raised his eyebrows. "I'm the police chief of a town who's had a murder and an attempted murder in the last week. I'm staying on this case."

"She's your sister. Do you really have the right to ignore that connection and how it might be affecting you?"

"It's a small town. We're all connected somehow. It wouldn't make sense for me not to be on it. And I don't technically report to you, I'd like to remind you."

Summer looked back at Erynn, exhausted but still awake enough to be slightly amused by the familiar tension and banter between her brother and the other law enforcement officer.

"Let's focus on your sister and not jurisdiction, alright? I'm sorry I said anything." She looked back at Summer. "Can you tell me what happened yesterday in your own words, starting from the beginning?"

"I can. You know about the break-in here…"

"It was more than that. It was attempted kidnapping," Noah interjected.

Summer shuddered.

"We all know, Noah." Erynn spoke softly, her eyes never leaving Summer. "Keep going."

Summer knew her brother was getting testy because he was so concerned, and appreciated Erynn ignoring his displays of crankiness. She also appreciated Erynn's quiet voice. Her head was starting to hurt a little. Lack of sleep and dehydration, she guessed.

With that in mind, she reached for the water bottle Clay had brought her before he'd been taken in another direction to give his statement. Summer wished they hadn't been split up, but she supposed she understood why they'd all want to talk to the two of them separately, see if their stories had any differences or if they'd both noticed the same details.

She took a long drink and then looked up. "Clay and I went to Anchorage because…" She hesitated. Neither of them was technically supposed to be investigating so she wasn't sure how to phrase what their intentions had been without giving that away. Noah had been the one to suggest they talk to APD, but Summer still feared if she phrased it wrong they'd know she'd been investigating. "We felt like the case had reached a dead end and hoped talking to the officers at APD might help, since they've been working the case longer." There, that was vague but true.

Erynn nodded.

"They had nothing and then we were run off the road while we were driving in Anchorage. We didn't feel safe staying in town so we headed back to Moose Haven. We'd been driving awhile outside Turnagain Pass—"

"Can you guess how far?"

"I'm not sure. We'd crossed Silvertip Creek but hadn't reached the Canyon Creek rest area yet. That's the best I can tell you." Even when they'd gotten into the car earlier, it had taken Summer about twenty minutes to focus and realize she should have been paying attention when they passed landmarks to give herself a better idea of exactly where they'd been. Thankfully if someone drove her back, she believed she should be able to pinpoint their location fairly accurately. Mountain trails tended to imprint themselves on her memory.

"That's pretty good. That's the area troopers went to just now after they got Clay's call."

Summer thought again about how he'd been genuinely concerned for the well-being of the man who'd been after them. Something about that messed with her mind. What a weird balance a man in his line of work—former line of work, technically—had to maintain, between justice and mercy. Summer wasn't sure she could keep both of them in mind like that so well.

"We'd slowed down, I think. I was asleep, but when I woke up we were almost stopped, so I assume Clay had slowed. There were construction cones, I do remember that, so maybe that was some kind of setup."

"Extremely likely, I'd say based on gut instinct, but we should know more when the team out there is finished investigating."

"The man shot at us, at the tires, I think, and then Clay told me to get out and run, so I did."

"And you ran for how long?"

"I have no idea. Miles? Hours?" She shook her head. "It's hard to think about either when you know someone behind you has a gun and wants you dead. Maybe Clay will know. I do know we stopped eventually, near a large canyon wall-type area of Six Mile Creek. Clay thought we should rest a bit, I think he'd planned on at least me getting some sleep, though that didn't happen. He was hoping to reach either the Hope Cutoff or the Seward Highway, whichever made more sense to get to, to get help."

"And you did, right?"

Summer shrugged. "Basically. But while we were stopped the shooter caught up with us and shot at us." She motioned to her leg. "That's when I was grazed, not when he shot at us on the highway." Frowning, she looked at Noah. "Where is the car anyway?"

"Troopers are going to retrieve it and take it to the state crime lab in Anchorage for processing. It's possible the killer could have done something to it while you were in the woods, and you know we don't have the capability to check for threats the way the state lab does."

"What do you mean? You've looked at it before," she reminded Noah.

"We've checked for signs of mechanical tampering, bombs. We looked for tracking devices once." Noah shook his head. "But I don't like how it seems like this guy always appears to know where you are. Either he has a source on the inside or he's tracking you somehow."

Summer understood. And shivered.

"Those are all the questions I have for now," Erynn said and looked at Noah. "Did you have any to add?"

"You covered it well." He looked at Summer. "I did get your text about the knife shop in Anchorage. Did you send that before you were run off the road?"

"Yes." She nodded. "A little while before. I'm not sure how long, but I didn't figure it would send until we were almost home. I just didn't want to forget to ask you."

"Well, I got it. And good thinking, but I called APD and they actually already checked out that guy. The knife shop was on their radar because of the weapon the killer has used. It may be from that shop, based on some evidence I can't tell you about, so they already checked him out and they don't believe it's him."

Summer didn't know whether she should feel relief

or not. On one hand, she was glad it wasn't that particular acquaintance, but on the other hand, her attempts to come up with a suspect list hadn't been very helpful.

And she was exhausted. Inside and out.

"Can I go sleep now?" Summer asked Noah, feeling like she was on the edge of falling apart emotionally, something she didn't want Clay to see. He'd seen her at her most vulnerable already, earlier when they were talking, and she needed to maintain just a little distance.

He nodded. "Yes. I'm going to stay close. I'll probably just sit in one of those chairs in your room once you fall asleep."

She wanted to ask if that was necessary, but knew that it was. Besides, after what had happened the last time she'd fallen asleep in her room, she didn't think she'd be able to rest peacefully without having someone there with her. So without arguing, she stood and walked to the stairs, then up to her room where she laid down in her dirty clothes and fell asleep within seconds.

FOURTEEN

When Clay woke from his nap the sun was high in the sky, not that that told him much about what time it was. He reached for his phone, which sat on the bedside table. Just past 2:00 p.m.

He threw back the covers, stretched and counted. Better than six hours of sleep, which was like gold in an investigation like this. Noah would have understood how much he was helping Clay by letting him take a break this long.

Clay took a quick shower and changed into clean clothes, then hurried down the stairs, wondering if Summer had slept, if she was awake yet.

She wasn't downstairs in the family's living room, so he headed out into the main great room of the lodge.

"How are you doing?" Tyler asked from behind the desk, coming around to look Clay over. "You look pretty good. No injuries that I can see. Why'd you let my sister get shot?"

"You know I'd have taken the bullet for her if I'd been given the choice." Clay said the words and meant them, realizing too late that the tone of his voice would probably convince Tyler all too well how much he meant them.

Sure enough, his friend studied him. "I asked for one thing."

Clay shook his head, ran a hand through his hair. "It wasn't on purpose, okay?"

"But you are falling for her."

Was he? Maybe. Yes. No. Clay just needed to keep them both alive long enough to find out. "I care. A lot." It was what he knew was true, so it was what he told Tyler. He didn't want to hide anything from his friend.

"She's been through a lot."

"I know."

"No, you don't know this part. There was a guy—"

"I know all of it."

Tyler looked at him.

Clay nodded.

"All of it?"

"Yes. I'm sure."

"Don't break her heart, Clay. That's all I ever wanted, was to keep her heart from getting broken. You're here for the summer and then what?"

"I'd planned to leave."

It was the worst time for him to catch sight of Summer coming down the main stairs, but there she was. Clay didn't know how much she'd heard. The last part without context sounded pretty bad. But he didn't know if he was ready for her to understand how much he felt for her. How dangerously close to crazy about her he was.

"You're leaving?" she asked quietly as she approached where the two of them stood.

Clay looked over at Tyler.

"Not right now," Tyler said. "I just meant he'd only asked for a job for the summer."

Clay watched Summer's defenses go up again and

wished he could do something about that, but having that conversation in front of her brother wasn't something she'd appreciate, he was sure.

"I've got to get back to work," Tyler said to Clay. "We'll talk more later?"

"Sure." He'd have agreed to almost anything to have Tyler leave so he could get Summer alone to explain. "How did you sleep?" he asked her.

"Pretty good. I woke up around half an hour ago and just laid there being thankful I wasn't in the woods anymore." She smiled a little. "Dry socks never felt so good, either," she added, holding up one wool sock–clad foot.

"I'm sure. I wanted to talk to you about today. Mind if we sit somewhere?"

"Let's go back to the family room." Summer led the way and they each took a seat on the sofa. She only sat two feet from him but it felt farther, with the way her arms were crossed defensively, shutting him out.

"I know you walked in on a weird part of the conversation I was having with Tyler." Clay had never been one to beat around the bush.

"You're leaving. I get it."

"Not now. And I don't know if I want to. Anymore."

She looked at him, then shook her head. "You've got to be a police officer again, Clay. You're too good at this to run from it forever."

"Who says I'm running?"

"Aren't you?" She met his gaze, level, looking more confident than she ever had. Because of how her story had drawn them even closer together?

Clay still wanted to talk more about that. The shooter had chosen the worst time to come after them, not that there ever would have been a good time.

"About the conversation we had…"

"Is it okay if I don't want to talk about it right now?" Her voice softened, making the words not sound harsh or demanding.

Clay could do nothing but agree. "Of course. The case? Can we talk about that?"

Unless it was his imagination, she relaxed a bit, leaning back against the sofa cushions. She grabbed a throw pillow from beside her and brought it into her lap to hold. "Sure. If there's any chance it will make this nightmare end sooner, I'm all for it."

Clay was too. He'd miss being with Summer every day but her safety wasn't worth extending his time with her.

"I was thinking about the man who is after you."

"Me too." Summer shuddered. "Almost every time I close my eyes."

"I'm trying to figure out who it could be. I think we should make a list."

"I don't exactly have a list of enemies, Clay." Summer shook her head.

"I know you don't. But someone is after you, and chances are good you've met them."

"Why do you think so?" Summer asked but immediately shook her head. "No, of course they'd have to know me. Unless he was just waiting on the trail for anyone, but if so it's entirely too coincidental that I share so many similarities with the other victims."

"Let's talk about them more."

"I wrote everything down in a notebook." Summer's eyes widened and she paled. "It was in the car."

Problems with that ran through Clay's mind in a line, one after another. They didn't have her notes, problem one. The *killer* might have their notes, problem two. The police might find their notes and know they'd been investigating. Problem three.

"I didn't write everything down. I tried to keep it pretty bare-bones just in case."

"Good thinking on your part," Clay said aloud, wanting to calm her down some as he could see her eyes widening. "Why don't we not worry about that right now. The police will bring our belongings back once they've processed them for evidence, and then we'll know if there's any fallout from the notebook."

She nodded. "Okay. I can do that. Not worrying. Much."

"Good. Now, what do we remember?"

"All the women were outdoorsy. That's the first thing that comes to my mind."

"If we assume that's the critical factor connecting the victims, where could he have met you?"

Summer held up a finger. "Hold on just a minute…"

She stood and walked toward the door. Clay followed her. He thought he heard her sigh and he understood— having personal security was restrictive to be sure. But it was necessary still and Clay wasn't going to take any chances.

She walked to the front desk and said something to Tyler. Clay wasn't close enough to hear—he thought she'd appreciate the slightest bit of space.

Tyler opened a closet that was to the side of the front desk, behind it. What were they up to?

He reached in and pulled out a whiteboard, and handed it to Summer. She smiled and turned back to Clay. A bag of dry-erase markers was taped to it. Smart. They could brainstorm and then erase the evidence so they wouldn't have a second notebook situation, something Clay appreciated. Even though he'd told Summer not to worry, he was still slightly concerned about the fact that the investigating they'd been doing might be made public.

They returned to the living room.

"Okay." Summer opened a marker and set the board in front of them, leaning it against the coffee table. "Places he could have met any of us."

"Hiking. That's the first and probably most obvious."

Summer nodded. "I agree. It's also the hardest to prove or to track down. It's not like most trails have any kind of log system and it would be almost impossible to get witnesses or really anything to back this one up."

"That doesn't mean it isn't a possibility."

"You're right, I suppose." She wrote it down. "What else?"

"Races? Have you run anything lately? Some 5Ks? Outdoorsy people are often the ones who do those too and I know Anchorage has a lot."

She shrugged. "I've done a couple this year. Could be." She wrote it down.

"What about a store for your equipment?"

"It's possible. I get most of my stuff at Anchorage Outdoor Gear, where we were, but I've gotten shoes at Mountain Central before." She wrote down the names of both stores.

"What else?"

"Trailheads?" she suggested.

"What do you mean?"

"What if he isn't a hiker but he fishes or something and that was how we crossed paths?" She shrugged.

"It's a stretch. It's basically the same as hiking, so I just thought I'd toss it out there."

"Go ahead and write it down," Clay suggested, and Summer seemed to agree. She nodded and set the marker down on the coffee table.

"Hiking. Races. Stores. Trailheads," he read aloud.

"There's no way to make a list from those things. There's no way to know who hiked somewhere at a certain time or shopped somewhere when I was there." She shook her head.

"Technically in a store like Anchorage Outdoor Gear we might be able to access online copies of receipts if we needed to prove you were there on the same day as someone else, but I see your point. We might be able to use it to prove a connection when we have a suspect in custody, but it won't help us narrow down a list."

"So we're at another dead end for now though." Summer didn't sugarcoat things, did she? While he wished he could soften the blow of what she'd already realized, Clay appreciated that about her.

"At the moment. But I think we're close."

"Why do you think so?"

He shifted his weight to face her and waited until he was sure he had her attention. "I think he is afraid you can identify him."

She stood. Paced. "Why do you think that?"

He stayed seated on the couch but watched her carefully, tensing every time she walked in front of a window. That might be an overreaction on his part—no one else involved in the investigation would agree with his tension there...but then again, no one else had seen how well the guy after them could shoot.

"He's changed how he's coming after you. That's unexpected. I think you have him rattled."

"But you saw the sketch APD did. He wore a mask, Clay, I don't know who he is."

"So maybe it's his voice that he thinks you could identify. But he wouldn't go to this much trouble to kill you if you hadn't become a threat."

"Isn't that the very definition of a serial killer? Someone who tries to kill other people?"

"Sure, but think about it. He killed those other women with a knife, the same way he initially tried to kill you."

She nodded slowly. "Okay. But he's not doing that anymore. And you think that's significant?"

"I'm sure it is. Serial killers fit a profile, they play by their own set of rules. Even though they obviously have extreme issues, what they do makes sense to them. They tend to follow patterns even more so than other criminals. He has broken his. It must be for a reason."

"I did notice things had escalated. Tracking me down to my home, almost being run off the road, being shot at multiple different times…"

"It's not about his usual motives anymore. Now he just wants you dead."

"Wow, don't beat around the bush at all, Clay."

"You can take it."

"What makes you so sure?"

"Because you're the strongest woman I know."

Summer didn't know how to react, not to Clay's words or his nearness. Sometime in the span of a few minutes he'd ended up shifting over to where she sat on the couch and now she was leaning in his direction. Eight more inches and she could kiss him.

Six.

Four. She held there, met his eyes and swallowed hard as she tried to decide what she wanted, what he wanted, what she was doing.

Clay lowered his chin, just slightly. But enough for Summer to tell that her unspoken "kiss me" invitation might be getting an answer.

She jerked backward. "We should go down to the station and tell Noah what we came up with."

Clay hadn't moved, hadn't backed up or apologized for his part in the almost kiss. Not that she wanted him to. Not that she wanted him to acknowledge it, either.

Summer stood, brushed her hair, which had fallen in her face as she'd leaned toward Clay, behind her ear and straightened her shoulders. "We'll drive your truck, then, right? Since my car is…"

"Yes."

She hurried outside, even more flustered by the calmness in Clay's voice. Did nothing rattle him?

Maybe not, and not that many things rattled her. But the way she still felt drawn to Clay, the way he still seemed like he might share those feelings even after she'd told him all she had…

Neither of them said much on the way into town, but much to Summer's surprise the silence wasn't awkward. Just full. Like there was so much to say and neither of them wanted to say it. Summer knew they'd eventually have to finish the conversation she'd started in the woods if there was ever going to be anything between them. Not that Clay had said there was, and besides, wasn't he leaving?

Summer walked with Clay into the building and took a deep breath. Reliving this over and over was getting a little easier, but that didn't mean it was objectively easy. The fact was she couldn't stop looking over her shoulder to see if anyone was watching, if anyone was waiting to attack. Because this was actually her real life. Where someone wanted her dead.

"Summer. Clay." Noah was walking past the door as soon as they walked in and immediately turned to face them. "Did you come to talk to me? I was just on the phone with the troopers and was about to call you. They recovered Summer's car. No indication it's been messed with since you left it."

She breathed a sigh of relief. Maybe that meant they didn't have to process the car's contents and no one would notice the notebook?

Noah frowned. "They wanted me to ask you why you have so much information about the case in a notebook?"

Summer looked at Clay. They both looked back at Noah but neither said anything.

"We'd better go to my office."

They followed him there. Summer ran her hand over her forehead, trying to do anything to ease the tension that had developed when Noah said they had the notebook. How did they explain that?

"Don't be mad, Noah," Summer said as soon as he'd shut the door behind them, before either she or Clay had even had the chance to sit down.

"I don't know what exactly I'd be mad about. I just don't understand why the two of you seem to be conducting some kind of unofficial investigation."

There wasn't much worse than getting caught doing something you weren't supposed to be doing. Especially by Noah. Because when he wasn't working, wasn't worried about a serial killer terrorizing his town, he was laid-back and funny. But the sense of humor all but disappeared under the pressure of the job.

"I'll explain," Clay started. Summer was more than willing to let him do so. She leaned back a little in the chair.

"We're not interfering," he continued, "and we haven't done anything illegal or unethical."

"Not telling me what you were up to dances close to both of those."

"Maybe it does. But it's not either one and I stand by that." Clay's shoulders were straight, his posture not defiant but confident. Summer cracked a tiny smile. Her brother was a difficult man to stand up to but Clay was doing an admirable job.

"Why don't you describe exactly what you *have* done, if you don't mind."

Summer held her breath. Waited.

"We sorted through some ideas we both had, and compiled them in the notebook."

"I wrote them down. That was my fault." Summer wasn't proud of it, but she knew that first of all, it was true, and second of all, Noah was much less likely to be upset with her than Clay, and for some reason, she didn't want him to have any reason to dislike Clay.

"What else?" Noah kept going.

Clay looked at Summer. She winced. This was where he was going to be the least happy with them.

"We talked to some people with…connections to the case and asked them some questions."

"You conducted unauthorized interviews?" Noah's eyes widened. He pressed a hand on his forehead, closing his eyes. Summer half wondered if he was counting to ten to calm himself down.

"Again—" Clay's voice was still steady "—we didn't do anything unethical. Unadvisable, maybe. But we just talked to them. Summer is the one who has the most in common with the other victims and we thought she might be able to find a connection that law enforcement officers might overlook."

"I don't know what to say to either of you right now." Noah looked between the two of them. "You." He focused on Summer. "You need to take your safety more seriously. And leave the investigating to the people who are in charge. And you." He fixed his glare on Clay, and Summer thought it was harsher than the one she'd gotten. "You should have known better."

"Than what? There's a serial killer still terrorizing south central, no law enforcement agency I've talked to is making progress and it's not anyone's fault because I've seen how hard people are working. I thought I might have found a way to make some progress."

"Involving my sister in an investigation you're supposed to be protecting her from?"

"I'm supposed to be protecting her from the killer. Not from a knowledge of the very real danger she's facing."

"I'd prefer she was protected from both."

Summer threw her hands up. "Stop, both of you. Please."

Both men looked at her. Though neither had been out of line and Clay had kept his usual calm tone, Summer couldn't take it anymore. "Aren't we all on the same team?"

"Technically I'm on a team with my officers here and the troopers, and my team is trying to keep you safe." He directed the words at Summer.

"Okay, then," she began, growing more frustrated

with her brother by the moment. "Doesn't that mean Clay is on your team?"

Her brother looked at the other man—and then his shoulders sagged a bit as the ire seemed to drain out of him. "Yes. He's keeping you safe, doing what I ask. Yes, he is. You're right, Summer." He studied Clay for another moment, then stuck out his hand. "I apologize. That was unprofessional of me."

Clay shook it. "I understand. I care about your sister too."

Noah nodded, taking the words at their true face value rather than reading into them like she suspected she would do in whatever few quiet moments she had for the rest of the day.

"The troopers will be bringing the car into town sometime tomorrow if all goes according to plan. They took it to Anchorage and the lab needs time to examine it."

Tomorrow? Summer wasn't counting on it. That seemed like an unrealistically fast turnaround and besides, plans didn't seem to mean much these days, not with the high stakes her life had turned into.

"Thanks." She smiled.

"I'd like to look at that notebook when we get it back, with your permission, Summer."

She knew he didn't have to ask and so she nodded. "Sure. I don't know what we have that could help, but if there's anything…"

"Actually I think we should tell him what we'd come here to talk to him about," Clay broke in.

"I'm all ears."

"I told Summer that I was thinking, sort of rolling

things around in my head about this case and realizing that the killer's MO has changed substantially."

"Not hard to notice."

"No, but I think it lets us make a few assumptions or at least gives us some conjectures and possibilities to investigate."

"Such as?"

"I think the killer believes Summer can identify him."

Noah's brows rose. "If that's true, then you realize security will need to be tighter."

Clay nodded and Summer frowned. They hadn't talked about this. What did he mean by that? More officers, or were they going to push the safe house issue? She couldn't imagine being stuck somewhere isolated without the freedom to hike and explore the mountains around her.

"We can talk about that in a minute. But as for the why, think about his MO. He's a serial killer, he does things with a purpose, deranged though it may be."

"I'm still following."

"And he isn't trying to kill Summer in his usual way anymore. He's realized he's probably not going to get that chance. But rather than give up on her entirely, he's fixated on her."

"Could just be some weird psychological obsession."

"I would agree if he kept trying to attack her with the knife that was used in the other murders. That's personal to him."

Summer felt like she was going to be sick, remembering the glint of the blade. Instead she drew a deep breath and focused on the patterns in the carpet while Clay kept talking.

"But you're saying that now his methods of attack are so impersonal you don't think his motives are the same."

Clay nodded. "Exactly. Now he just wants to eliminate her. He's acting like he views her as a threat."

Summer looked up from the carpet long enough to chime in. "But I don't know who he is, I really don't." She shook her head. "I've thought through almost everyone I know who hikes, random people I've seen often on the trail who might fit the build, on Facebook groups. I've got nothing."

Noah blew out a breath, slowly. "Okay. If that's true, and I think you have a good reason for believing that it is, how does this change our investigation? Where should we be looking differently?"

"I'm not sure it gives us any clues in that direction but it does give us some ideas about how he might continue to operate," Clay offered.

"How?"

"He's going to hit hard and he's not going to stop until either he is captured or Summer is dead. Because at this point, he believes he has nothing to lose."

FIFTEEN

Past one in the morning and Clay couldn't sleep. The sky outside had finally darkened to something that resembled nighttime, but still he couldn't shut off his thoughts. His body was exhausted despite the rest he'd gotten earlier in the day, but his mind refused to follow suit.

He turned over again. Glanced at the clock one more time only to find less than one minute had passed. Noah was on watch now, since Clay had agreed to take the first sleeping shift. They were switching at two.

An hour to sleep.

He turned over again and closed his eyes. They snapped open and he threw back the covers. Gas. He smelled gas.

He grabbed his jacket on the way out of the door of his room, thankful he'd slept in all his clothes.

Noah met him in the hallway. "I smell gas downstairs."

"I just smelled it too. Where's Summer?"

"Her room. I'll get her." Noah threw the door open and ran inside. Clay waited in the hall but was ready to take Summer's hand as soon as she came out. Noah hurried ahead of the two of them. "Get Summer outside!"

"What if it's a trap?"

"It's a risk we have to take." The other man's expression was grim. Clay ducked back into his room, grabbed his handgun from the bedside table drawer and tucked it into the side of his waistband, then took Summer's hand again.

He and Summer ran outside, the cold wrapping like an unwelcome blanket around them. He felt Summer shiver and wished he'd taken the time to grab his jacket so he could offer it to her.

Tyler and Kate both ran out only a minute later. Kate was carrying an extra jacket. "I wasn't sure you'd have gotten yours," she said to Summer as she handed her one.

Summer smiled, something that surprised Clay a little. "That's my always-prepared sister."

"How are you smiling?" Kate shook her head, looked at Clay. "Does she not get it?"

"Get what?" Summer asked.

Clay didn't know. She didn't seem nearly scared enough to understand the full range of danger they could be facing even now.

Worst-case scenario now that they were outside and presumably safe was that the gas smell was some kind of trap to get them outside so the killer could pick Summer off. It wasn't a scenario Clay wanted to consider but it had the potential to be the very one they were facing, so he made sure he stayed on alert, looking in multiple directions. There was enough light to make out shapes, a dim sort of twilight, but so far nothing looked out of place to him.

"You don't get that this is really bad!" Kate frowned, her frustration obviously overcoming her vocabulary in Clay's opinion because *bad* didn't begin to cover it.

"I haven't exactly thought a guy after me was good. Ever."

"No, but you're not taking it seriously. I heard Noah talking last night, again, about how you'd be better off in a safe house." Kate threw her hands up. "What else needs to happen to convince you to listen to him? He's not just your brother, he's the chief of police here and if I were you I'd do what he says."

"I don't want to leave you guys, leave the lodge with no one to lead the hikes."

"Someone's trying to kill you and you're worried about leading hikes?" Kate didn't bother to hide her disbelief.

"I don't want to hurt the lodge."

"We don't want *you* hurt. That's what matters most." Kate glanced back at the building. "But if you don't want to hurt the lodge, consider what happened tonight. That's certainly not helping it."

Summer's smile fell from her face, her shoulders slouched as the reality of the danger sunk in. Clay wished Kate had been more careful with her words—Summer already carried so much guilt. But gentle or not, she was right.

Summer looked at Clay. Then back at Kate. "Alright. I'll do it."

Kate nodded once. "Tell Noah when he gets out here."

No one said anything after that. Kate had killed any kind of optimism Summer had been showing. While Clay wished he could see her smile again, he knew that right now she needed the reminder of the seriousness of the situation.

If they'd been trapped inside, if the gas had kept leaking, they could have succumbed to carbon monoxide poisoning. It was also possible that whoever caused the leak had intended to set off an explosion.

That scenario was probably the deadliest. Thankfully it hadn't happened.

But it could have.

The building alarm went off. Clay wondered if the CO detectors hadn't detected a problem until then or if Noah had had to set them off manually.

It didn't take long for the guests who were staying at the lodge to start filing out, most in what looked like pajamas and bathrobes. All of them looking understandably upset.

Clay hated to admit it but the safe house was looking like the best option to him too. Not just for Summer's safety, although that was his top priority, but for the safety of those around her, like Kate had pointed out. If the worst had happened tonight, the death toll would have been extreme, and would have included far too many innocent people who had no involvement in this case at all. This wasn't something they could handle in the same way they'd been trying to. It was time to admit they needed another plan. There, standing in the darkness, he felt like he'd failed somehow. Yes, Summer was still alive, for which he was thankful, but he hadn't been able to handle keeping her safe on his own. He hadn't been able to eliminate the threat completely.

He hated when it felt like the bad guys were winning. He knew that, thanks to God and His plan, evil never won in the end. Ever. But sometimes on earth that wasn't how it felt. And it grated against his sense of justice, against all the reasons he'd become a cop after high school in the first place.

I don't know how to handle this, God. Help.

Noah stepped out of the building. Shook his head.

And Clay knew it was good that Summer had decided about the safe house on her own because at least she'd feel better about it that way.

Because he was pretty sure Noah was no longer giving her a choice in the matter. And Clay didn't blame him. Whoever was after her wasn't stopping. And her life was growing more dangerous every day.

When the Moose Haven Fire Department finally left, having declared the building safe, Summer was still standing in the parking lot, staring at the lodge. A light rain had started to fall as dawn broke across the sky, but she didn't care. Let the rain fall.

She had to leave.

Summer wished tears would come, anything to give her some way to work through the overwhelming wave of emotions crashing against her right now, but none did. She just stared ahead, aware that Clay was close by talking to some other police officers, that her siblings were nearby. And yet, she'd never felt more alone in her life.

She'd fought for her chance to lead the hikes at this lodge, and she'd checked as recently as last week—occupancy at the lodge was up since she'd started doing them. Summer didn't know why people seemed to care so much about whether or not she was there. She was a has-been mountain runner, but that one season she'd spent in Europe, even placing in some races, had helped her make just enough of a name for herself that it appeared she really was good for business.

And now she had to leave. Because rather than helping her family's lodge recover from economic setbacks, her presence was hurting it. Of course that was the secondary reason she was leaving—hers and everyone else's safety being the first priority. Still, she felt the sting. For the first time since the man had grabbed her in the woods, Summer let a dark thought flicker through her mind.

Was this all punishment for the way she'd lived a few years ago? For the choices she'd made?

She let the thought linger. Considered it.

"Summer?"

She blinked. She'd almost forgotten she wasn't alone because it felt very much like she was. She looked at Clay.

"It's me, you and Noah. And we need to leave as soon as possible."

Summer nodded, looked back at the lodge and wished one more time for tears that didn't come. "I'll go pack."

Not long after, Summer had her turquoise backpack strapped to her back and was dressed for hiking. After feeling so overwhelmed earlier, she felt strangely calm now that they were about to drive to the trailhead for their family's cabin, the location they'd decided made the most sense as a safe house. She had failed in how she wanted to help her family, for now. But that didn't mean this was the end. Once the danger was over and she was able to come back, she would do better, try harder, somehow make the lodge work and make up to her family for how she hadn't been there for them in the past.

The ride to the trailhead was quiet. Neither of the men seemed like they were in a talkative mood and Summer definitely wasn't, so no one spoke. There was no need to talk as they began hiking, either. Summer and Noah both knew where they were going and Clay just followed close behind.

How much longer was this going to last? Summer wondered as she pushed her pace faster, not from any sense of danger but because she needed to feel her muscles burn, needed to feel alive. She'd always loved the way hiking focused her, making her feel like if she could conquer this hike she could conquer anything. But today, the hike wasn't enough to clear her mind. How much longer would she have to live like this, with someone after her?

She kept putting one foot in front of the other. The next right step, the next right thing, just like the pastor of the church in town her family attended had told her to do when she returned to town and wanted to know how to make things right with God, with her family.

The next right thing with her family had been to stay at the lodge, devote herself to helping it succeed. At least, that had been the plan.

The next right thing with God?

Summer had never stopped long enough to figure out what it was. Only knew it was there, hovering just out of her reach and feeling like if she just tried hard enough, focused hard enough, she'd know. Whether or not it would be something she'd be willing to do, she wasn't sure. But right now she didn't even know what it was.

Thinking in that direction made her feel unsettled, a feeling she'd had quite enough of lately, so she turned her thoughts to Clay.

He'd said nothing about her past, about the conversation they'd shared. Of course when had he had the chance? They'd been too busy reacting to events they couldn't control.

Summer flinched when she thought that. Was that what her life had been the last three years? Just a chain of reactions to events because she knew she wasn't ultimately in charge of her life and so she felt perpetually like she was spinning out of control?

Oddly enough, except on ridgelines.

Summer exhaled, managed to stop thinking so much, stop analyzing as she continued to hike through the trees. They broke through the tree line after about forty-five minutes of hard hiking, and then they were on the edge of the mountain, taking the trail that led straight up to the ridge, which they'd travel for another half a mile before reaching their family's cabin.

It was the best possible place for a safe house because they could see the trail to it clearly over a considerable distance. Anyone coming would be obvious because the cabin sat at the end of a ridge. To approach it from any other direction, avoiding the path, would take climbing skills that few people had.

When Summer was up on the ridge her thoughts drifted back again, pounding in her heart to the rhythm of her quickened heartbeat.

Up here, what Jenna Hunt's mom had asked for felt easy. Up here, she could feel alive, even now. The irony got to her, but she couldn't explain it. How could someone who wanted control so desperately possibly feel the best up here, at the mercy of nature?

Because the ridgeline was a visible reminder that she wasn't in control. That life wasn't about that, wasn't about risk management.

It was about…life.

Abundant life.

Summer stopped, there in the trail. Looked up at Noah, but he didn't turn around. Turned back to Clay, but he just frowned like he was worried about her. "You okay?" he asked after she'd been staring at him for a minute.

Abundant life. Where had that idea, which felt almost like a correction to her thoughts, come from?

She looked out over the landscape of the Kenai Peninsula beneath them, breathing deep as she surveyed the green of the trees in the valley below, the ethereal blue-green of the river below and then Seal Bay off in the distance, and the town of Moose Haven.

Then her eyes looked out farther, to the next mountain range. Ridges, valleys, endless nothing, and Summer felt like she always did on a ridgeline. So very small.

You are so big, God. So much more powerful than I am.

The admission was the first prayer she'd prayed in years that hadn't been asking for something, the first attempt at conversation she'd made with her Creator since she'd walked away from what she'd believed.

Summer started walking again. She didn't want the men to have to wait for her, and she knew they must both be on edge with them so exposed at the moment, outside of the relative safety of the cabin's walls.

But as she walked, she kept praying.

Did You remind me about that, about abundant life? Because I know You're right. Life isn't the point, not even living it to the fullest, though I think that's better than not. But You want us to live to the fullest not just for those we've lost but for You. As a way to thank You for this world, for the ridgelines, for the valleys, for all of it.

Tears stung in her eyes. For innocence lost. A baby whose tiny feet had melted Summer's heart, though they would never walk on earth. For the family she'd gotten back but had held at arm's length.

For her relationship with Jesus. Which she'd pushed away or ignored for so long that it felt like a natural re-action. Much more natural than this looking around, praying, praising.

"Do you want to be made well?"

Summer recognized the quote, from somewhere in the New Testament. Jesus had asked that of a woman when He'd walked the earth.

Was He asking her that now? Or was her mind just recalling Scriptures it had known in the past?

Either way, Summer nodded, felt her chest tighten a little and then release, her shoulders feeling lighter than they had in years.

"Yes," she whispered to God as she looked out over the mountains He had created. And still created her. "Yes I do."

SIXTEEN

The cabin was the perfect safe house. Clay had seen as soon as they'd begun their approach down the ridgeline why Noah had been so sure they had the best possible location in mind. Egress would be almost impossible without detection.

He and Noah had talked while Summer was packing, working out logistics. Noah had a SAT phone with him, since regular cell phones wouldn't get service this far from a tower, and he'd call the Moose Haven PD to keep in touch with the other officer there to see if any progress was being made. They both voiced the hope that maybe tampering with the gas lines at the lodge would be where the guy would mess up, that maybe he'd made some kind of mistake that would result in him finally getting caught.

But neither of them was counting on that, and they'd made plans for who would take which watch, what to do in case of several contingencies. Clay felt they were as well prepared as they could be. Having at least one more officer would have been ideal, but there just wasn't the manpower to spare. Even two men were more than was practical, but this was Summer and no one was taking chances with her safety.

Ten feet from the cabin Noah stopped hiking and turned back. "Stay with Clay," he told Summer.

She did so and Noah went inside to clear the building, though they had no reason to believe the killer would have been able to anticipate them coming up here.

Clay's only concern was the fact that this cabin wasn't a secret. Noah insisted it wasn't extremely well-known, but the fact was that *someone* might know, and Clay didn't want their location to somehow make it to the attention of the man who wanted Summer dead.

He had the uncomfortable feeling that he might be wrestling with some trust issues. But it was a valid question his heart couldn't stop asking—Why was God letting Summer be stalked by this man? Why wasn't He helping the police find his identity so they could eliminate the threat by putting him behind bars where he belonged?

Clay had seen enough evil in police work that he'd already worked through questions about injustice, about why God let bad things happen to good people. But it didn't stop a few persistent, unanswerable questions from popping up now and then. Clay asked them when they came though, knowing that ignoring them wouldn't help and wouldn't strengthen his relationship with God the way the hard stuff did, much as he didn't like going through it at the time.

"Are you doing okay?" Clay asked Summer quietly. He'd prayed for her, especially on the hike up this morning. The things she'd been through... He understood more after hearing part of her story why she struggled with faith the way she did, even though he knew God hadn't abandoned her.

"I'm okay."

"Seriously?" Clay wanted the real answer, not to just be brushed aside. Besides, if she wanted to back off a little from their growing friendship, she'd picked an impossible time to do it. The three of them were going to be stuck in a relatively small cabin indefinitely.

"All clear."

Not that Noah being with them would give Clay and Summer much time to talk privately.

Clay followed Summer to the cabin. The front was a wide deck that looked out over the landscape below. There were four steps up to the deck. The front door was off the deck—Clay hoped there was a back door because while having only one entrance and exit meant less places to protect, it could be bad if they needed to escape in a hurry.

He leaned back around the side of the house. The windows were wide enough to serve as exits if there were an emergency, something Clay was hoping to avoid.

He stole another glance at Summer. Despite her initial protests, she looked more relaxed here at the safe house than she'd looked in Moose Haven for a while.

Clay felt relaxed up here too, like it was easier to see clearly on the top of the world.

For the first time since he'd left Treasure Point, he could think through that situation, analyze what he'd done wrong—the mistakes that had shaken his faith in himself as an officer of the law. And he came up with…

Nothing. Well, almost nothing. He should have listened to Kelsey, his cousin, when, months ago, someone had been trying to kill her and she'd had suspicions that someone in their police department was the would-be killer. That had been his only mistake. And while it was a big one, nothing else had indicated who the traitor was.

There had been no clues. Thankfully, Kelsey was okay, and didn't blame Clay for not believing her gut instinct.

The man who had tried to kill her bore all the blame, she'd told Clay. Clay hadn't done anything, which was what grated him so badly. He hadn't done anything. But still, the situation itself, his cousin being in danger…

It hadn't been Clay's fault.

Somehow a weight lifted, he felt even lighter. Then looked up at the sky.

Did You allow those things to happen so I'd end up here? Do You sometimes allow something we view as bad because of the fact that You are working all things for our good?

The questions he asked God didn't have immediate audible answers. But something that felt a lot like peace edged over his heart.

He looked back at Summer. Tried to exhale some of his worries about her safety.

You're taking care of her too, in this situation, right, God?

Yes. God was in control, had His good purposes in mind. Clay just had to learn to let his trust rest firmly on Him.

Summer took a sip of coffee and winced. She hated coffee, but mornings in the cabin were cold if no one had kept a fire going overnight, which none of them had because the weather hadn't been forecasted to be especially cold.

Well, the weather hadn't gotten the memo. All of her was cold, down to her toes. She shivered, then took another sip of the nasty brown liquid some people apparently liked. Noah watched her with amusement. Clay was still sleeping since he'd taken the first watch last night.

She was about a third of the way through the coffee when Clay walked out. "Is that coffee?" He raised his eyebrows. "I thought you only drank tea?"

Summer sputtered a little, having attempted another sip. "I'm freezing."

Clay smiled and shook his head, then reached into his backpack and pulled out a box of Irish breakfast tea. "I'm sorry I wasn't up sooner. Want to trade?"

Before she could stop him he'd started heating the water. She watched as he steeped the tea for her, finding something spellbinding in the fact that the same hands that were prepared to defend her from any threat were now gently making her tea. It seemed so domestic and such a contradiction but also so *Clay* that she just smiled.

She took the tea from him, handed off the coffee and sat in the silence, feeling for half a second like she could imagine a future like this. Her and Clay as…something. Friends? More? They would have to see, but she wanted him in her life.

Wanted a life like this. With some peace. Rest.

Summer glanced out the window. They were on top of a ridgeline. That summarized her desires for life well, didn't it? Rest on a ridgeline.

"I've got to call Moose Haven in a minute so I may step out onto the deck," Noah said to Clay, glancing at Summer as he did so.

So much for her few minutes of peace. Everything about the investigation slammed back into her mind, creating dark corners and shadows and worry where a few minutes ago there had been quiet and calm.

If Noah was concerned about her trying to overhear

his conversation, he didn't need to be. Summer was done with interfering. She'd tried to get involved, tried to help with the investigation and do some good, and it hadn't helped. If anything, it had hurt. They were no closer to finding him than she'd been before she stepped out of her comfort zone and tried to do something that made her feel less like a victim.

So maybe it was time to sit back and acknowledge that she was out of her depth here.

Clay looked over at her. She could tell he wanted to say something. Amazing how well you could learn how to read someone else's facial expressions when you were with them almost constantly.

Noah went outside, shutting the door carefully behind him.

"Are you okay?"

Summer looked at Clay. "I'm not sure."

"Why?"

"I…" Her mind felt like it was spinning. She'd felt so good only a few minutes before but right now the weight of her situation was pressing on her and she couldn't handle it. Was this what a panic attack felt like? Summer struggled to shake it off, but nothing helped. She looked down at her hands. They were shaking.

She shrugged.

"Hey." He set his coffee mug down, reached out for her hands and took them both. "This will be over soon."

She didn't know if she didn't believe the words or if she was worried it was true, that it would be over soon in a way that would mean the killer had succeeded in—

"I'm not going to let him get to you."

Clay's words were quiet.

Summer nodded. Looked out the window as she replayed the conversation she'd had with Mrs. Hunt. *Really, truly live without regrets.*

The desire to do that wrestled with the unexpected fear that had found her two nights ago at the lodge when there had been the gas leak. For some reason it was that incident that had gotten her attention, more than any other attempt the killer had made on her life. Maybe because it hadn't just been her in danger. It had been innocent people.

"So what's the plan?" Summer asked after taking a long sip of tea to steady herself. It seemed to work at least a little.

"We wait." Clay's face sobered.

"For him to come try…"

Clay shook his head. "No. It's a safe house. There's no sort of plan to use you for bait, Summer. We don't anticipate this place being compromised at all. We're just waiting for a break on the case."

"How can anyone get that if he doesn't try anything else?"

"They're still working on the previous crime scenes. It's not as fast as the movies make it seem—there are other crimes to investigate, other work that has to be done, and most of it is manual, done by actual people."

Summer sighed. She didn't like seeming high maintenance but it seemed like there had to be a way for things to go faster. Waiting had never been a strong suit of hers.

Noah walked back in then, the SAT phone in his hand.

"Any news?" She hated how eager her voice sounded.

He shook his head. "Nothing. I'm afraid we're going to be up here for a while, so I'm going to go get some firewood."

"I'm in favor of that. I'm not drinking coffee again tomorrow."

"I'll be back soon." He looked at Clay. "Take care of my sister. I shouldn't be more than an hour."

And then Noah was gone again.

Summer looked over at Clay, feeling his eyes on her. "What?"

"You won't have to drink coffee ever again if I can help it." He smiled.

"I didn't say thank you...for bringing the tea." She blushed a little, suddenly self-conscious of the nice thing he'd done for her, and the fact that they were alone.

And that he knew her deepest, darkest secrets and still seemed to care...

"Summer, something you said when we were running near Six Mile Creek..."

Her body stiffened. She looked down, then felt Clay's hand on her right shoulder. Felt a soft squeeze, brotherly almost.

But when she looked up at him and met his eyes. There was nothing brotherly in the gentle expression he was giving her.

"You are that kind of woman. You're the kind who goes through hard things and comes out stronger. You still have your childhood faith, I can tell by the way you talk about what happened. If you didn't believe in God, still have a relationship with Him even if it's messed up right now, you wouldn't care so much. You are stronger than you realize, and you can be more than you imagine. It's up to you."

He exhaled. "That's all I wanted to say. I just didn't get a chance the other day and it has bothered me ever since to think of you wandering around with such a low opinion of yourself. Seeing yourself that way."

She laughed, but it was without humor. "I do see myself that way. Every single time I look in the mirror."

"I'll never see you that way."

Their faces drew closer. Summer didn't know who moved first. All she knew was that he was close enough now that she could see the stubble on his jaw, the roughness contrasting with the smoothness of his lips, which were close enough for hers to brush over.

Summer closed her eyes and let her lips find his. And let him convince her with his kiss.

SEVENTEEN

So the timing could have been better, since they were in a safe house and everything in Summer's life was so uncertain. Clay still wanted to be careful, and he didn't want it to seem like he was taking advantage of her vulnerability, even a little, but she'd kissed him first. He'd just finished it.

And then he'd pulled away, like the gentleman his mama had raised him to be.

"Clay..."

He smiled, brushed a hand along the edge of her jawline, so softly it felt like he'd barely touched it. "I care about you, Summer. A lot. Enough to tell you that I'm not going to complicate your life more than it is now by making promises or plans. But when this is over..."

She nodded. Smiled just enough that Clay had hope that, even though she wasn't vocalizing it right now, maybe she felt the same way he did.

He stood and walked to one of the windows, feeling like he should give her a little space, though it was hard in a cabin this small. He glanced at his watch. Forty-five minutes since Noah had left. He'd said he'd return within an hour. Clay didn't think Summer had noticed how much time had passed yet, so he left the subject alone. She didn't need to add any worries about her brother to the ones he could already see she was carrying.

Although something had seemed to lessen that weight a little since the hike yesterday. She seemed different somehow, her face a little lighter. But she was still carrying a burden on her shoulders. Her past? The killer? Clay didn't know which. But he wished he could fix it for her.

Instead he prayed, knowing God could handle whatever it was. And then he made her another cup of tea because it was always nice to do something tangible too.

She took the tea with a smile, then it flickered away into a frown. "How long has Noah been gone? It seems like it's been a while."

Clay hesitated before answering. He looked at his watch again. "Just short of an hour."

"You've got to go look for him."

"He's not late yet."

"He said within an hour," she argued. "He wouldn't have said that if he didn't mean it."

Clay shook his head. "He may have misestimated. He'd have had to hike back down to the tree line for firewood and that may have taken longer than he expected it to."

Her expression made it clear she wasn't comforted. "And he may have walked into some kind of trap."

Clay looked out the window. The sky was a cloudless blue. After taking so long to get to the Kenai, the summer weather seemed to be showing off for them. The early morning chill was probably gone too. There was no visible reason it should have taken Noah longer than he'd planned.

But Clay wasn't leaving Summer. That wasn't even

an option. And taking her with him back down the exposed ridgeline wasn't a good idea in his opinion, either.

"You've got to find him, Clay." Summer had come up behind him and he turned to face her, already shaking his head.

"I can't, Summer. You're my first priority."

She didn't argue but her expression made her thoughts clear. Another stretch of time passed. Noah was now half an hour later than he should have been.

"We've got to do something," she muttered, looking at Clay with such a wide-eyed look of desperation that he nodded.

"I'll use the SAT phone and call the Moose Haven Police. Maybe they can send someone up just to double-check." It would extend the circle of people who knew where they were, which was something they'd taken great care to avoid, but it was the best option he had.

"Thank you." Summer's voice was quiet.

Clay made the call, gave them the location where Noah should be and also called Tyler at the lodge to let him know. It didn't seem fair for him to be kept in the dark.

"Thanks, man." Tyler's voice was genuinely appreciative.

"You'd do the same for me," Clay said.

"I would. You take care of my sister, okay?"

"I'm not planning to let anything happen to her."

"I mean…I mean more than that." Tyler sighed. "I'm trying to tell you if you want to pursue her, if you really do know everything that happened and you feel like you can treat her like she deserves, you have my blessing for what it's worth."

Clay smiled. Maybe a little late considering that kiss,

but he appreciated knowing his friend wouldn't have a problem knowing he'd fallen in love with his sister. He'd truly only been trying to protect her. "Thanks, Tyler."

He hung up the phone and filled Summer in on everything except what Tyler had said about the two of them. It wasn't the time for that.

He noticed her looking out the window while he talked and finally asked her what she was looking at.

"It's so sunny…and yet, did you notice it getting hazier out there?" She sniffed the air. "And I smell smoke."

Clay shook his head. "I don't smell anything."

She leaned closer to the window, then turned and walked to another one. "I'm sure, Clay. That's where it's coming from, the smoke. Look."

He followed her and looked where she motioned. There was smoke, billowing from somewhere just behind the cabin. Maybe from the cabin itself.

Options seemed limited at that point. He ran through them, discarding them as he went. Bringing Summer with him to check out the fire was a bad option. Leaving Summer alone in the cabin was a bad option. Both of them staying in the cabin was a bad option.

If this wasn't an accident, wasn't a patch of dry grass that had sparked somehow…

The chances of it being a natural, accidental fire seemed slim. Lightning was rare enough in this part of Alaska, and when you added in the fact that the sky still had hardly a cloud, nothing that would indicate lightning…

If the killer wasn't out there, Clay had no idea what had happened.

But if it was the killer, then he had them. Checkmate. Clay couldn't let the two of them burn to death up there, knowing they hadn't even tried to fight.

"Okay, Summer, listen to me."

"This is really bad isn't it?"

She had paled and Clay grabbed both her upper arms, gently but with enough firmness to get her attention. "I need you to look at me. I need you to stay focused and I need you to be the amazing, tough mountain runner you always have been and conquer whatever this situation is becoming."

"Is he out there?"

"I honestly don't know."

"But you're going to go see."

He nodded as he removed his weapon from his holster. "I'm going to leave this with you."

"You can't go out there knowing there may be a killer with nothing to fight with, Clay."

"I can't leave you without anything, either."

"You have to. I've got bear spray, but you have one chance at eliminating the threat before it gets to me and that's the goal here, right? I think that is the best option."

Clay nodded. He couldn't argue with the facts she'd presented and all things considered it was probably the best choice of two less-than-perfect ones.

"Stay in here. And stay safe." He took one long look at her, wishing he could kiss her again but knowing that there wasn't time. The smoke was growing thicker. And the threat was growing.

He shut the door and walked onto the deck. The smoke smell in the air was thicker out there. He walked down the steps, awareness heightened, ready to respond to any threat he saw with his .45 out and ready to fire. He kept it angled down slightly at the ground as he ran around the side of the cabin. Nothing there, but yes, the cabin was on fire. Ironically it looked like it had started on the outside of the chimney on the back of the cabin. Clay moved his feet slowly, picking his steps with care as there wasn't much room between the back of the cabin and the cliff off the back of the ridge.

He looked at the fire. Too much to handle with the water they'd brought to drink, but he could try. Maybe use some dirt too...

If all else failed, he'd get Summer and they'd head down the mountain as soon as possible. He'd run anywhere on the planet if he needed to, or hole up anywhere he could find if it would keep Summer safe. Either way.

He just needed her to be okay.

Clay turned to go back inside and alert Summer that possible threat or not, they were going to have to evacuate. But he hadn't moved from where he stood before he saw something out of the corner of his eye. Someone.

And before he could react, something hard hit the side of his head.

Clay was taking too long. There was no way around it and Summer was facing the truth. Noah was gone. Clay was gone. It was extremely likely that she was next.

Summer paced the cabin, walked by another window and looked out. She didn't see any signs that someone other than the three of them had been up there. Even the smoke could still possibly be an accident. Or, well, it could have been if both men hadn't disappeared.

At this point, Summer had very little hope that this wasn't a very intentional setup.

She needed a plan, that much she knew, but she had no idea how to go about coming up with one. Fight back. That was the best plan she had. Why had she insisted

Clay take that gun? She hadn't heard it go off, so he hadn't used it.

Summer had bear spray, but it sprayed in such a wide arc that she knew it would get in her eyes too, especially inside a room like this where it lacked the open air to disperse and she'd also be at the mercy of the super-powered mace.

She looked around for something else she could use as a weapon. Anything else.

And the door creaked open. Her shoulders sagged with relief as she closed her eyes and let out a breath of relief. One of them was back.

But they didn't say anything, and even though only seconds had passed, she would have expected Noah to immediately explain where he'd been and Clay to tell her where the smoke was coming from.

Summer opened her eyes.

The man in the doorway was backlit by the sun, but after she blinked a few times she figured out how the form was familiar and identified the only vaguely familiar face. "Wait…"

"Hello, Summer."

"I know you." She squinted, still trying to place him. "You work at Anchorage Outdoor Gear. Ryan, right?"

He only stood and smiled as he gave a nod at his name, not moving an inch.

"But why are you here? You're not…you're not…"

But as he continued standing silently, that smile sending chills up Summer's spine, she realized that yes, he was.

As an employee of one of the best outdoor stores in Alaska, he'd had access to all of the women. They were outdoorsy types; they'd almost certainly all shopped at his store. And the reason she knew his name wasn't just because of his name tag, he was also part of a Facebook group for hikers.

Summer swallowed hard. She hadn't thought to look, but she was sure now that if she got online and looked at the members, every one of the victims would be on the list. Many people posted photos of their favorite hikes, shared trail conditions.

Whether he'd chosen his victims on that Facebook group or at the store, it made sense.

It was him.

"You're the killer."

EIGHTEEN

Clay had the worst headache of his life, but it was the least of his worries. He hadn't gotten a look at the guy who'd hit him, but he was at least Clay's size, maybe bigger, and in good shape. Summer wouldn't stand a chance in a hand-to-hand fight.

The side of his head where he'd been hit throbbed. He'd blacked out for a second or two, and then he'd opened his eyes but stayed still as the guy walked away from him. Clay had known that headache or no, he wasn't fast enough to get past the man and get back inside to Summer first. So he'd have to let this man make it into the cabin and get distracted by Summer. It was the only chance Clay would have for taking him out. He was counting on the fact that this was the serial killer, and that since he had Summer alone he planned to take his time, like his usual MO, and not just immediately eliminate her.

It was a risk, but it was one Clay had to take for Summer's own good.

Now he crept along the side of the cabin, listening. He heard Summer's stunned voice as she realized the identity of the killer. She was quiet for a few seconds after that, and Clay wondered if she was figuring out how it had all worked, how the man had met her and the other victims. It was clear she knew him and he thought he'd heard her say something about an outdoor store.

He took a quick glance in the window he was crouching under. Summer was standing at the rear of the living area of the cabin, her back to a wall. The man was at the door, barely inside.

As far as Clay could tell, he didn't have a firearm on him, but he wasn't willing to bet their lives on that. If Clay chose the wrong time to attack him and this man did have a gun, everything would escalate too quickly for him to keep the situation under any sort of control.

At least he had a gun he could use if he needed it, though he couldn't in good conscience take the guy out when he was just standing there. But if it was clear he was trying to kill Summer, and Clay could get a shot…

He felt his hip for his weapon. Closed his eyes tight and rubbed his head.

The holster was empty.

The killer must have taken it when Clay blacked out. Had it been longer than a second or two? But if it had, why had it taken so long for the other man to walk away from him? And why hadn't he shot Clay?

He knew he might not get answers to those questions even if the guy ended up in police custody. Sometimes there were no answers.

Knowing the killer had Clay's weapon changed the plan. Now he had to wait for just the right moment. He'd only have one chance.

And if he picked the wrong time, they'd all end up dead.

"You're on that hiking Facebook group, aren't you?" She was surprised at how the question came without hesitation. Her voice wasn't even shaking. It was like Summer was watching herself from somewhere outside her body. Shouldn't she be too scared to speak?

She didn't know. All she knew was that she was terrified, sure, but she was also mad. How dare this man steal the lives of those other women? How dare he try to steal hers, both by trying to kill her and by making her too scared to do the things she loved and enjoyed?

Really live.

That was what she wanted to do. Really live. And she was sick of this man getting in the way of that. Tired of the lack of justice.

"I'm surprised you figured that out." The look of admiration he turned on her had an element of creepiness that did make goose bumps run down her arms, but she kept staring him down. Summer had no idea where this bolder version of herself had come from, but she felt more like the Summer she'd been before she'd run away with Christopher. Before…everything.

But it wasn't just that. She felt like a stronger, braver version of that woman.

Is that because of You, God?

She didn't have time to wait for an answer to her quick prayer. She took a deep breath and stared at him. "So you watched people's conversations to learn where they would be and found places to lie in wait for them." She didn't bother to hide her disgust and his expression twisted slightly. It bothered him that she was disgusted. Interesting.

She'd stopped posting her favorite hikes on that site last year, stopped posting anything other than the occasional unlabeled picture after Noah found out and told her that it wasn't safe to give complete strangers so much information. He'd said it wasn't just because she was a woman who often hiked alone, but also that her name recognition played into it.

She'd agreed and stopped posting.

But it had apparently been too late. She'd already said too much.

"So that's how you knew where I'd hike." She restated it, piecing the other elements they'd wondered about together in her mind as they came to her. "How did you know exactly where I'd be the other times? When you tried to run us off the road, when you shot at us..."

He laughed. "GPS tracking really has come a long way."

Of course. The Anchorage Police Department still had her car, but as far as Summer knew they hadn't been able to process it yet. She was sure they'd find the tracker, but knew that it wasn't suprising that Moose Haven hadn't been able to. They simply didn't have the resources to scan for trackers electronically and the new ones were so tiny and so easy to hide that it wasn't something they'd have been able to readily identify even in a thorough search.

"How did you find this place?"

He shook his head. "Small towns talk. It wasn't too hard to find out your family owned more property than just the lodge."

She wanted to ask him about his background, to see if he had spent time in the military or hunting, the way Clay had suggested, to become such a good shot. But she didn't know if it was better to keep him talking or to start trying to figure out exactly how she was going to get out of this alive.

Because she *had* to get out alive. The edges of her

eyes stung and she blinked, refusing to show any sign of weakness. She hated feeling like prey. Animals in the wild chose the weak ones, the ones with wounds to attack. Any sign of weakness attracted predators.

While she didn't for a second believe that this human predator had chosen his victims with any kind of logic—none of the women had done anything to deserve his fixation, his desire to see them dead—she still refused to give him the satisfaction of seeing her afraid.

Even if the thought of dying, of not seeing Clay again, made her throat tighten until she could barely breathe. She wanted to look into his eyes again, see him smile. Tell him that if she was going to live her life to the fullest, really live, then she wanted him in it. Tell him she loved him. Hoped that maybe she'd hear the words back.

Where *was* he? Understanding hit her hard. There was a good chance he was dead. Though she hadn't heard gunshots, there were many ways to kill someone, and if Clay was alive he wouldn't let her face this man alone.

God, help him please. Don't let him die. Or me.

She turned her attention back to the killer. Frowned a little as a thought crossed her mind.

He was wounded somewhere, wasn't he? Summer knew Clay had hit him with one of his shots only a few days before, which meant Summer had that on her side. If she could figure out where it was.

"You're going to die today, Summer Dawson." He moved toward her slowly, catlike in the way he prowled along the edge of the room toward her rather than walk straight in her direction. She shivered, not liking the feeling that she was being toyed with.

Of all the ways he'd tried to kill her, this one, this up close and personal slow death, was her least favorite.

And Summer wasn't going out like this.

She took a deep breath. Watched him. His right shoulder. Was it her, or was he holding that oddly, like he was more conscious of it? Could that be where he was wounded?

She waited as he walked toward her, prayed he'd continue circling her rather than stop in front of her. She glanced down at her foot quickly, then back up at him, calculating exactly where she'd need to kick to hit him the hardest.

He shifted his weight to the left, exposing his shoulder perfectly.

Summer kicked fast and hard. He yelled.

Seconds passed in a blur, flashes of activity catching Summer's attention. The man's screams, him clutching his arm. Footsteps, coming from somewhere.

Then Ryan was on her, grabbing her arms, rage evident as he channeled all his strength into fighting her. Summer tried to fight back but he was enormous compared to her. For an instant she felt like she understood what had gone through the heads of the women who had ended up dead at Ryan's hands. Fighting was useless. Futile.

But no, it was the only choice she had. She struggled, punched him in the nose, kneed him like she'd seen Sandra Bullock do in a movie once.

He shoved her hard against a wall, and then advanced toward her. Summer stood tall, readying herself for whatever blow was coming next but knowing she couldn't take many more. She could already taste blood on her lip.

The front door slammed open.

Clay was there. Within seconds he was inside, taking Summer's place and drawing Ryan's attention to himself. The two men were fighting and Summer backed away, experiencing the first small taste of freedom and glimmer of hope she'd felt since Ryan had burst into the cabin. She watched the men fight, wondered how she could help Clay. He was hurt. He had a long, deep gash on the side of his head. She winced—he'd been hit by something. A rock? That could explain why he hadn't come back when he should have and why she hadn't heard anything.

Smoke billowed through the open front door, and when Summer looked back she realized the back wall of the cabin had flames growing, from the base of the wall near the fireplace.

Ryan had set the cabin on fire?

Ryan.

She turned her attention back to him, found Ryan and Clay still fighting. Ryan had an inch or so on Clay, but Clay hit hard. It hadn't taken him long to discover the spot where Ryan was wounded, either, and Summer could see he was focusing his hits on Ryan's right side.

Summer ran to the front door and pushed the door shut since more smoke seemed to be coming from outside than from the fire inside. She didn't want them to die of smoke inhalation before they had a chance to end this. She knew they didn't have long before the entire cabin was in flames but she didn't know how long. It was fire-treated wood but it wouldn't withstand direct fire for long. Seconds? Minutes? She wasn't sure.

She hurried back to where the fighting was taking place, did her best to stay out of the way. Maybe she should run? But no, what if Clay needed her later?

He was starting to seem unsteady on his feet, she noticed, but she couldn't tell why. From what she could see, Clay seemed to be getting in the best hits.

But still, he stumbled backward. Summer rushed toward him, not sure how much help she'd be but determined to try.

The door slammed open again and relief almost overwhelmed Summer as she caught a glimpse of her brother Noah, still alive after all. Summer looked back at the killer, watched as Ryan's attention went to the door. Ignoring the throbbing in her foot, she landed one more hard kick against his shoulder. As she did so Clay seemed to gain just a little more strength and no sooner had she kicked Ryan than Clay landed one last punch, directly on the side of the man's head.

He fell to the ground, unconscious.

Everything stilled. Summer took a breath, listened to her heart pounding and looked around the cabin. "We've got to get out of here."

The back wall was engulfed now, flames dancing and advancing toward them.

"Noah," Clay called to the other man. "Summer, get out."

She wanted to argue but Clay's tone made it clear that wouldn't go over well. She went to the deck, which was as far as she dared go in case they needed her help, and waited, holding her breath almost from fear, for them to come out.

We're alive, God. You did it. You saved us.

She swallowed hard. God wasn't finished with her, wasn't ignoring her because she'd made mistakes. Wasn't punishing her.

Forgive me, Lord.

Just when she was about to run back inside to make

sure her brother and Clay both got out, they came through the door, dragging Ryan behind them. They'd handcuffed his hands together.

Noah nodded behind him. "The SAT phone. It's on the counter."

Clay ducked back inside. Summer didn't think she took another breath until he emerged.

There he was safe. Both of them safe.

He tossed the phone to Noah. "Call the troopers. We need to get this guy off the mountain."

NINETEEN

The troopers had managed to get a helicopter close enough to get Ryan loaded into it. He was on his way to Spring Creek Correctional Center in Seward.

He wasn't going to take any more innocent lives.

Clay finally took a deep breath when that man was gone from the mountain, out of their lives. Summer would have to testify, more than likely both of them would, but that wouldn't be for months or years to come. For now, it was over, and for today that was enough.

The remains of the cabin were burning down behind them. Emergency personnel had decided the best course of action was to let it burn, since it was surrounded by rocks that wouldn't be able to spread the fire. Unfortunately saving the cabin itself would have required too much resource-wise, and the cost and risk would be higher than it was worth, especially since the scene would be compromised anyway from a crime scene perspective.

Clay had detected a note of relief on Summer's face when that decision had been made.

"I'd rather our family rebuild anyway. Start over."

The words had seemed to carry a double meaning for

her that Clay suspected had something to do with how she felt she'd let them down. Did that mean she wasn't holding the past over her head anymore?

He wasn't sure. But he walked over to her now, to where she stood a safe distance back watching the flames finish the work Ryan had started. The sky overhead was still blue and cloudless, the air warm. It was a gorgeous summer day.

A day for new beginnings.

Clay took Summer's hand in his. "Are you okay?"

She turned to him, glacier-blue eyes clear. "I'm better than okay." She sniffed as she wiped what he thought might have been the remains of a tear from the corner of her eye.

"Want to take a walk down the ridgeline or did you want to stay here?"

"A walk would be good, I think."

Hand in hand, they walked back toward the trail where they'd come up. Had that just been yesterday? The last twenty-four hours had seemed like days, moving slowly and quickly all at the same time, so packed full of changing and near-death experiences.

Clay reminded himself to take a deep breath. It was over, the danger, the case. And hopefully, he and Summer were just beginning.

"I noticed this spot yesterday, when we hiked up here." He looked at Summer. "I thought it was the most beautiful place in the world."

She smiled up at him. His heart caught.

"And I think you're the most beautiful woman I've ever seen." Clay was surprised at how easily the words came. They were true. He felt them with everything in him. "And if everything that happened to me in Treasure Point had to happen for me to get here, to meet you, it was worth it."

Summer squeezed his hand, and somehow it meant more than sentences full of words ever could have. She understood.

"I know…" Clay cleared his throat, tried to breathe around the tightness in his chest. It wasn't every day he asked a woman to marry him and he wanted to do this right. He'd already messed up by not having a ring ready, but he'd learned from the last week that life was short. Some risks were worth it, and loving Summer, asking her this question today, here on the mountain where they'd both been given a fresh start, it was worth everything despite not being perfect.

Because she was. Perfect for him. He hoped he could be half the man she deserved. And if she said yes to his question, he'd spend the rest of his life making sure he was.

"I know we haven't known each other for long. And I know everything has been crazy. But I also know I love you, Summer."

"I love you too."

The words, said quietly but with certainty, relaxed the tightness in his chest. He tightened his grip on her hand. She squeezed back and he turned to face her, lifted a hand and stroked her cheek. "I want to spend the rest of my life loving you."

Her eyes widened. Hopefully in a good way. Clay kept talking. "I want to marry you, Summer Dawson, and live up here with you, having adventure upon adventure, watching you run up mountains and along ridgelines. Would you be my wife? Will you marry me?"

She laughed, full hearted, her eyes shimmering with so much hope Clay felt it too.

He brushed a tear from her face. A happy tear, the only kind he ever intended to be the cause of for the rest of their lives.

"Yes, Clay. I would love to marry you."

He wrapped her in his arms, squeezed her in a tight hug and then released her just far enough back that he could tip his head down and claim her lips in a kiss.

Their happily-ever-after was just beginning. And Clay couldn't wait to see what their future held.

* * * * *

*Don't miss Sarah Varland's other exciting
romantic suspense stories:*

*TREASURE POINT SECRETS
TUNDRA THREAT
COLD CASE WITNESS
SILENT NIGHT SHADOWS
PERILOUS HOMECOMING*

Find more great reads at www.LoveInspired.com.

Dear Reader,

Welcome to Alaska! While I love Georgia, where I was born and where I've set many of my stories, Alaska is my favorite state and I had so much fun setting a book in areas that are familiar to me. While Moose Haven is purely imaginary, if you ever find yourself in Alaska and can make it to the town of Seward, which is near Moose Haven in this story, I think you'll find it's pretty similar. I'm looking forward to returning to Moose Haven soon for Tyler Dawson's story.

Writing about Clay Hitchcock was so fun for me because he's been with me for five books now. When he first had a small side character part in my debut novel, *Treasure Point Secrets*, I knew I liked him. Summer was such a fun contrast to him and I enjoyed imagining their story.

Both main characters in this story struggled with some amount of guilt: Clay for feeling like he let down his fellow officers in Georgia; and Summer for the way her past actions had impacted her family. Guilt is a powerful thing, but God's forgiveness is stronger. They both also struggled with grief, and Summer especially wrestled with how her grief had taken some of the fullness out of her life. I loved writing the hints in this book to Summer about how Jesus wants us to have an abundant life because those words are so true for us who are real people. Grief is difficult to work through, but I believe God still wants us to live abundantly, to be thankful for our lives and to hold on to hope.

Along those lines, in this story, I finally came right out and touched on the subject of miscarriage. If, like me, you're one of the women who has lost a baby and needs someone to talk to, please know that I would be happy to chat by email. Also know that you are not alone. And that God is still love, and still faithful.

Hearing from readers is one of my favorite parts of writing and I'd love to hear from you! You can get in touch through email at sarahvarland@gmail.com, or find me on Facebook at Facebook.com/sarahvarlandauthor.

Sarah Varland

COMING NEXT MONTH FROM
Love Inspired® Suspense

Available March 6, 2018

LOOK FOR THESE AND OTHER LOVE INSPIRED BOOKS WHEREVER BOOKS ARE SOLD, INCLUDING MOST BOOKSTORES, SUPERMARKETS, DISCOUNT STORES AND DRUGSTORES.

LISCNM0218

Get 2 Free Books,

Plus 2 Free Gifts—

just for trying the Reader Service!

YES! Please send me 2 FREE Love Inspired® Suspense novels and my 2 FREE mystery gifts (gifts are worth about $10 retail). After receiving them, if I don't wish to receive any more books, I can return the shipping statement marked "cancel." If I don't cancel, I will receive 4 brand-new novels every month and be billed just $5.24 each for the regular-print edition or $5.74 each for the larger-print edition in the U.S., or $5.74 each for the regular-print edition or $6.24 each for the larger-print edition in Canada. That's a savings of at least 13% off the cover price. It's quite a bargain! Shipping and handling is just 50¢ per book in the U.S. and 75¢ per book in Canada*. I understand that accepting the 2 free books and gifts places me under no obligation to buy anything. I can always return a shipment and cancel at any time. The free books and gifts are mine to keep no matter what I decide.

Please check one: ☐ Love Inspired Suspense Regular-Print   ☐ Love Inspired Suspense Larger-Print
                         (153/353 IDN GMWT)   (107/307 IDN GMWT)

Name _____ (PLEASE PRINT) _____

Address _____ Apt. # _____

City _____ State/Prov. _____ Zip/Postal Code _____

Signature (if under 18, a parent or guardian must sign) _____

Mail to the **Reader Service:**

IN U.S.A.: P.O. Box 1341, Buffalo, NY 14240-8531
IN CANADA: P.O. Box 603, Fort Erie, Ontario L2A 5X3

Want to try two free books from another line?
Call 1-800-873-8635 or visit www.ReaderService.com.

* Terms and prices subject to change without notice. Prices do not include applicable taxes. Sales tax applicable in N.Y. Canadian residents will be charged applicable taxes. Offer not valid in Quebec. This offer is limited to one order per household. Books received may not be as shown. Not valid for current subscribers to Love Inspired Suspense books. All orders subject to approval. Credit or debit balances in a customer's account(s) may be offset by any other outstanding balance owed by or to the customer. Please allow 4 to 6 weeks for delivery. Offer available while quantities last.

Your Privacy—The Reader Service is committed to protecting your privacy. Our Privacy Policy is available online at www.ReaderService.com or upon request from the Reader Service.

We make a portion of our mailing list available to reputable third parties that offer products we believe may interest you. If you prefer that we not exchange your name with third parties, or if you wish to clarify or modify your communication preferences, please visit us at www.ReaderService.com/consumerschoice or write to us at Reader Service Preference Service, P.O. Box 9062, Buffalo, NY 14240-9062. Include your complete name and address.

LIS17R3

Looking for inspiration in tales
of hope, faith and heartfelt romance?

Check out **Love Inspired**® and
Love Inspired® **Suspense** books!

New books available every month!

CONNECT WITH US AT:

Harlequin.com/Community

 Facebook.com/HarlequinBooks

Twitter.com/HarlequinBooks

 Instagram.com/HarlequinBooks

 Pinterest.com/HarlequinBooks

ReaderService.com

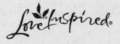

LIGENRE2018